# HAWKE'S NEST

BY

DARCY FLYNN

# Acknowledgments

It's so much fun for me to write a story set in one of my favorite places on earth, the Florida Panhandle. The Emerald Coast is one of the most beautiful beaches in the world. With the exception of my Tennessee farm, there's no place I'd rather be. Thank you Tom for making those delightful visits possible.

And thank you to my wonderful editor, Ally Robertson. Your detailed and insightful critique made my story even better. It was a pleasure working with you.

Thank you, Cindy Brannam for your thoughtful input into my story. I can always count on you. I love our brainstorming sessions and I would hate to be on this road without your friendship and support.

For Roman

# Chapter One

"You've *got* to be kidding me!" Annie Dell's gut churned at the sight of the blue lights flashing in her rear-view mirror.

First the delayed flight, then the mix up with the rental car, and now this. She slowed, eased off the road, then stopped. Her heart thumped as the patrol car pulled behind hers.

"This. Can. Not. Be. Happening."

She jerked her purse into her lap and slid out her driver's license. Shifting in the car seat, she tried to relax. She blew out a breath and glanced at her watch. Five forty-five. No way was she going to make it on time now.

She rolled down the window and peered into the side mirror. She watched the Franklin County Sheriff unfold from the car and amble to her door. *That's right. Take your time. I have no place to be.*

Annie gazed up at the face of the man dressed in green. A handsome, suntanned *god* stared down at her.

"Driver's license and registration, please."

She handed over the documents. She usually credited herself with some sense, but because she was in a hurry, a bit of cajoling might do the trick. She bit her lower lip and stared at his goofy green hat. This should be easy. She knew she was pretty, beautiful to some. At least that's what the photographer from the *Vogue* shoot told her last week. Gushed, was more like it. He was young, new with the magazine, and hadn't yet acquired the confidence of the more experienced photographers. He'd practically 'darlinged' her to death.

The stern expression on this officer's face told her he might be a tough sell, but he was a man, wasn't he? And in her experience, they all wanted the same thing. She flashed him her most beguiling smile, then topped off her soft sell with the slight bat of her long lashes. It was hard to tell if her mild flirting was having an effect, since department issued sunglasses concealed his eyes.

Wishing she'd taken the time to apply lipstick at the Hertz counter, she parted her lips ever so slightly and waited for his reaction. Stoned faced, he simply stared down at her. Her smile usually wreaked havoc on most men, but obviously not him. What was he, Robo Cop? His expression was wooden and with that bronze tan of his, she could almost believe he was.

"Ma'am, I clocked you going twenty-three miles over the speed limit. Is there an emergency?"

*Twenty-three miles?* Her mind raced and apparently so had her rental car. She'd had no idea she was going that fast. Could her day get any worse? "Well, sort of. My plane was late and I have a very important appointment. If you could just give me a warning this time, I'd be *really* grateful." She pressed her hands together like she was praying and gave him what *Glamour Magazine* called her sparkling cover girl smile.

He slowly slipped his sunglasses from his face, revealing the most remarkable blue eyes she'd ever seen. "How grateful?"

Annie almost choked. A chill crept up her spine. Suddenly, she had his undivided attention and wasn't sure she liked it. He didn't say another word, just stood there, eyeing her like the cat that had most definitely cornered the mouse.

"Um, what?" Her heart thumped in her chest.

"You said you'd be grateful." His mouth lifted at the corners. "How grateful?"

His eyes held a question. A question she could swear he already knew the answer to. They also said, *gotcha.*

Thumpity, thump. Her heart hammered like an irritating woodpecker against her ribs. But when those blue orbs casually raked over her face, landing on her chest, the knot in her mid-section kerplopped and her mouth went completely dry. She licked her lips. And her mind went blank, like an erased white board at the end of a school day.

"Well, I mean. Um." A warm flush filled her cheeks as the officer stared down at her. Except for the times she stood in fear before her father, she'd never been speechless with anyone. But, this man? He was something else. The chilling effect he had on her was tangible.

"Look, I'm very late. Just give me the ticket, will you?"

"This will only take a moment." His voice reverted back to that irritating *officer* tone. Then he turned to walk back to his squad car.

"I'm sure he has no place to be, except maybe a donut shop," she mumbled, peering at his retreating figure through the side mirror. Broad shoulders, a narrow waist, and lean hips walked away from her. "Well, maybe not donuts."

Annie drummed her fingers alongside the steering wheel and glanced at her watch. Finally, after what seemed an eternity, the officer approached her car. His long strides and athletic physique shouted sheer masculinity.

*Sheesh. Get a grip, Annie. It's not like you haven't been around a good-looking guy before.*

He leaned forward, tilting his head near her window. "Slow down, miss. Your safety is far more important than any appointment. But if it makes you feel any better, I'm now late for mine." With the flick of his wrist, he tore the ticket from his tablet and held it out to her. Smarting at his reprimand, she suddenly felt small and ridiculous. In her industry, a well-placed feminine wile was all it usually took to get her way. But this man would have none of it. He must be made of stone. She glanced up at his face. The firm set of his square jaw told her that no amount of pleading, cajoling, or eye batting would ever move him. If she'd paid better attention, she would have known this and saved herself the humiliation.

She took the ticket and stuffed it, along with her license, back in her purse, then tossed the registration on the passenger seat.

After checking the traffic, she pulled back out on the highway. Now, she'd be late for sure. As she headed down the highway, she noticed he was traveling behind her. She squirmed in her seat and tightened her hands on the wheel. Hopefully, he'd pull off at the next exit. She licked her lips and glanced at the odometer. Fearing she would speed again, she crept along the highway like a tortoise.

"Slow and steady wins the race." *Don't let him rattle you.* She passed an exit and he still cruised along behind her. "What is it with this guy?" A shudder ran through her. Her stomach churned. *Why doesn't he pass me?*

Nothing for it, she'd have to phone Liddy. It was evident this pokey speed was all the traction she was going to make. Annie pulled her phone from her purse and punched in the number. Before the third ring the blue light was flashing behind her again.

She pressed 'end' and pulled over. Something between anger and fear filled her as she watched him unfold his tall frame from his squad car. Years ago, she'd sworn to never let another man intimidate her. She sucked in a deep breath, determined to speak her mind.

Moments later, he stood at her window.

She held up the phone and waved it in his face. "I just want you to know that I'm one second away from calling 911. Your behavior is bordering on harassment."

"Are you aware we have a hands-free law here in Florida?"

His deep blue eyes bore into hers until she had no choice but to lower the phone to her lap.

"No." She clamped her teeth together.

"Driver's license and registration, please."

"Can't you just give me a warning?"

He shook his head. "Sorry, ma'am."

*If he ma'ams me one more time…*

Annie yanked her wallet out of her purse and handed him her license. Snatching up the registration from the seat next to her, it was all she could do not to throw it at him.

She crossed her arms and waited. This weekend was supposed to be fun—an escape from New York, the paparazzi, and the madness of being paired with Alex Langdon and his fraudulent activities. For the past two weeks, she'd been hounded and harassed by the media until she thought she'd scream. And now, this.

When he returned and handed her another ticket, she wanted to cry. There was no point in trying to argue with this man. He was robotic, cold hearted. The Buford Pusser of Florida.

# Chapter Two

Levi took the next exit after Annie Delany was well on her way. There was no need to tail her anymore. She'd certainly gotten the message. Loud and clear. He'd made sure of that.

Another fall break, self-absorbed daddy's girl who thought she could flirt her way out of a speeding ticket hits the dust. Good. Maybe he'd succeeded in keeping this one alive.

Levi unlocked the door to his apartment with just enough time for a quick shower and shave before heading to the Sea Breeze.

Stepping out of the hot steam, he wrapped a towel around his waist, then picked up the old-fashioned shaving soap and brush. The mug had been his grandfather's, but the brush was new. He'd bought it on a recent trip to

New York to see his father. He loved the old way of shaving. His grandfather had been a barber in a small town in South Georgia. He used to love visiting him in the summers and going to the shop with him. Loved watching him cut hair and shave the chins of the local men. Saturday mornings were always his favorite. The men hung around for hours, taking their turn in the chair and talking politics. Things he was too young to understand at that age, but the banter and camaraderie between the men had enthralled him.

He circled the brush over the bar of soap until it foamed, then slathered the white cream along his jaw. Tilting his head, he placed the blade to his cheek and slowly scraped his flesh.

As he slid the razor across his jaw, the image of golden brown eyes and a dewy complexion floated before him. He paused and rinsed the razor. Miss Delany didn't know it, but when that dimple appeared next to her mouth, his stomach had dipped and turned like the first fall on that mega roller coaster at Disney World. As he raised the blade to his neck, he thanked the Lord he was no longer a rookie, or he'd have let her off for sure. It wouldn't have been the first time shining eyes and an adorable smile knocked him off his feet.

He rinsed the blade, slung the excess water into the sink, then began scraping his neck. He wasn't sure why, but she'd annoyed the hell out of him. And it wasn't as if she was the first to try to get out of a ticket, so why the heck did she make him so angry?

He stopped shaving and rested his hands on the edge of the sink.

From the moment she'd raised her lovely eyes to his, fluttering those inky long lashes, he'd been fascinated. And when the corners of her pink mouth lifted in that exquisite smile, he'd been mesmerized.

Floored.

Knocked completely off his guard.

Frankly, he hadn't thought of anything else since he'd pulled her over. That was one of the reasons he'd tailed her afterward. Something about her got to him. And he was frustrated with himself because in that very moment he had been tempted, for the first time in years, to let this one go.

*And would she be dead, too?*

His chest tightened. He curled his hands into fists and stared at his reflection.

"She's way down the road now, so get over it."

Taking a deep breath, he raised the blade and gently pressed it to the other side of his face. Shelving those thoughts, he had to remind himself that he was immune to the sparkling eyed, smiling young women that sped, literally, across the path of his radar. With one last stroke of the razor, his five o'clock shadow disappeared.

* * *

Annie dragged her suitcase through the airy lobby of the Sea Breeze Hotel, stopped in front of guest registration and waited. She glanced from her wristwatch to the brass call bell on the counter in front of her. Just as she raised her hand to give it a light tap, a smiling young woman dressed in crisp white stepped from around the corner and greeted her.

"Checking in?"

"Yes."

Annie waited with growing impatience as the young woman chatted amiably while processing the registration, informing her about the area restaurants, beaches, shopping, and transportation. Any other time, she would have been delighted to hear about the local color. But all she wanted now was a quick getaway and a hot shower. She scribbled her name across the bottom of the registration form, took the key card from the clerk, and headed to the fourth floor.

Five minutes later, she stood motionless underneath the shower spray, eyes closed, and let the hot stream flow over her neck and shoulders. The image of masculine lips clamped tightly in aggravation taunted her. Her eyes flew open. Her neck muscles tensed, and a knot formed in the pit of her stomach. *Hateful man.* Stalking her like that. Riding her tail. She had half a mind to report him.

She got out of the shower, snatched up the towel and dried off. Getting dressed quickly was not a new experience for her. High fashion runway work required it. The turnaround time to get back on the runway with a completely new outfit was critical to the success of any good model. But when it came to a special occasion, she liked to spend more time getting herself together. But due to the day's events, that was not to be.

Again, the sexy Robo Cop came to mind. What was with her tonight? It wasn't like she hadn't run into his kind before. Handsome, way too sure of themselves, arrogant jocks that made you want to sock them in the nose. Damn, she was rattled. How could she let this oaf get to her like this?

Or was she actually angry because he'd called her bluff? No one had ever done that before. It usually took very little to get whatever reaction she wanted from the opposite sex. Not that she was proud of it. But it was something she'd had to learn at a young age in order to survive.

*Breathe, Annie, and get the heck ready.*

She slipped on the terrycloth robe provided by the hotel, then carefully applied her makeup. No way could she show up looking like a street urchin. Liddy would kill her. She smiled in spite of her angst. Sweet Liddy. Her dearest friend since grade school. She couldn't have made it these past months without her.

Annie stepped into her slinky blue dress and shimmied it over her hips. With the stress of having her face plastered on every TV and print news outlet the past two months, she had lost more weight. It was terrible to be continually paired up with Alex like she was some criminal because of her relationship with him. Sure, they'd shared an apartment, but they hadn't shared a bed. Not that many in the news would even know that. It was none of their business and she and Alex let them think what they liked. He was simply her protection and she his alibi, his excuse, and his reason for keeping fortune-hunting women from his door.

But, as the media was prone to do, they'd jumped to conclusions. When she'd voiced her concern, Alex had laughed and said *let them*. So they'd been paired together on many occasions. At the time, she'd had no idea he was swindling his clients. But, that fact somehow got lost in all the news coverage. She was culpable because she'd dated him. Overnight, she'd gone from being America's *darling* to Alex Langdon's *accomplice*. So, she'd packed her things and left, hoping the paparazzi would leave her alone. But no such luck. They'd continued to hound her, parking outside her apartment at all hours. Following her everywhere she went. It had been a nightmare.

Truthfully, she was heartbroken. The ignorant remarks from strangers on the street and the cruel commentary from most of the major news outlets were devastating. Talking to her therapist had certainly helped, but it was Liddy who had saved her. Liddy's constant calls, emails, and showing up on her doorstep that had gotten her through.

Now, it was Liddy's time, her turn to be the focus of their friendship. This weekend belonged to Liddy. After that, she'd have two weeks to unwind and work with the local girls involved with her charity. Two blessed weeks free of cameras, flash bulbs, and whispers at her approach.

Annie took one last look in the mirror and hurried out the door. The small ballroom was on the second floor of the hotel. She descended the stairs, careful not to snag her high heels on the cement steps.

She pushed open the heavy metal door and entered the carpeted hallway, then stepped across the short pile of carpet to the ornate teak doors marking the entrance to the ballroom.

White tablecloths, shimmering like pearls, adorned the round tables scattered throughout the intimate space. Twinkle lights, draped along the ceiling, added to the fairytale atmosphere and immediately calmed her harried state. She paused, enjoying the beautifully lit room. Votive candles nestled amongst pink sweetheart roses—sterling flatware and glistening china greeted her. Annie spotted her charming, vivacious friend on the opposite side of the room and headed toward her table. The candlelight brought a warm glow to the smiling faces seated around them. The entire scene was magical and certainly every bride's dream.

Liddy jumped up as Annie neared the table, laughter in her sparkling, light blue eyes.

"There you are," she said. "Thank goodness. I was beginning to get worried."

"I know." Annie opened her arms to receive Liddy's ferocious hug. "I should have called you. I'm sorry."

At five-foot-eight, Annie towered over her small friend. Even Liddy's three-inch heels couldn't make up the difference. The phrase *small but mighty* came to mind as Liddy ushered Annie over to Mark, her fiancé, who stood when they approached. Mark was tall, with wavy blonde hair. He clasped Annie's hand between his own.

"Hi, Annie. Liddy's told me so much about you. It's great to finally meet you."

"You as well," Annie said.

"Annie, this is the rest of our party. Beth Turner, Macon Brown, and Eddie and Kathie Cummings. Everyone, this is Annie De—"

Annie cleared her throat and gave Liddy a meaningful stare.

"Dell. My dearest friend and my maid of honor." *Sorry,* Liddy mouthed as she took her seat.

Annie knew it was silly, but for just a few days she didn't want to be Anna Delany. Top, New York, fashion model. She wanted to simply be Annie Dell, Liddy's maid of honor.

Annie smiled at the curious faces staring at her and sat down. Was it her or was everyone tentative in their greeting? Did Liddy's near slip give anything away? She wasn't sure. They seemed friendly enough, but since Alex's arrest, she was constantly second-guessing everyone's motives and actions. Slanted eyes. Smirks. Shuttered glances. She would never get used to them. And she was never prepared for the hurt they inflicted.

"That's good. Sit right there. The seat next to you is for Mark's best man. It seems Levi's running late as well. Which is highly unusual for him." She turned to Mark, who had also taken his seat. "Don't you think, sweetie?"

"It is. But he sent me a text. He'll be here soon."

Liddy turned back to Annie with large questioning eyes. "So tell me, what kept you? What happened?"

"You wouldn't believe it if I told you."

"I'm all ears, girlfriend."

"I was pulled over. Not once, but twice!" Annie shivered. "I got two tickets."

"For speeding? You?"

Annie rolled her eyes. "Yes. The second time for using the phone. I had no idea Florida was hands-free."

Liddy's eyes widened. "Mark, honey, Annie got stopped on her way here from the airport." Liddy chuckled. "Twice."

"Oh, you think it's funny do you? Well, believe me it was nothing of the sort. The man was obnoxious, rude, overbearing, impolite, hate—"

"Okay. We get it. Take a deep breath and eat your salad."

Annie inhaled slowly and looked down at the small white, gold-rimmed plate in front of her. The leafy greens and fresh plump shrimp beckoned her to partake, but frankly, after reliving that awful memory, she'd just about lost her appetite.

She glanced at her friend who was eyeing her with the expression of one who knew her well. "Okay." She smiled. "But only for you. I'm still in a foul mood if you must know, but I'll shake it off for you."

"You'd better. Now forget about your bad day and look forward to the best weekend of your life. I can't wait for you to meet your wedding date. Tall, silent, brooding. You know the type. And completely gorgeous."

"You sound like you have a crush on him." Annie chuckled.

"Nothing of the sort." Liddy laughed. "But wait 'til you meet him. You'll see what I mean."

"If he ever gets here." Annie had just forked a shrimp when Mark waved to someone at the other side of the room.

Annie swallowed her shrimp and reached for her wine. Taking a sip, she glanced up as Mark stood to introduce his best man to the others seated at the table.

"Everyone, this is Levi Hawke, not only my good friend and man of honor, but a trusted civil servant of Franklin County."

Annie almost spewed the wine from between her lips.

"Levi, this is Annie Dell, my maid of honor and your date for the weekend," Liddy said.

She could hardly breathe. A nightmare. That's what this was. An utter…complete…nightmare. Standing before her, dressed in a suit that fit his irritatingly, gorgeous physique to perfection, was Robo Cop.

She went rigid and stared up at the man looking down at her. His dark blue eyes flickered annoyance, his clenched jaw a sure sign he found the situation just as distasteful as she did. Tension oozed from every pore in his muscular body.

She dropped her eyes just long enough to settle her nerves, then glanced back up in time to acknowledge his brief nod before he took his seat next to her. Mouth suddenly dry, she took a sip of water, then sat in awkward silence. She could not mess this up for Liddy. Preoccupied, she pushed her salad around her plate, waiting for the butterflies and her mounting anger to subside. She had to regain her composure, and quickly, or Liddy would suspect something.

"I'm glad to see you arrived at your *important* appointment unscathed," Levi said.

The deep resonance of his voice did little to unruffle her feathers. If anything, it made it worse.

"I did, thank you." Her stilted tone was not only foreign to her own ears, but to Liddy's as well, if the look on her friend's face was anything to go by.

Annie attacked the bread plate with vigor, snapping up a hard roll. When she tried to spread a cold pad of butter across the crusty mass, it broke into pieces, flaking all over everything but the bread. Giving up, she turned her attention to a large shrimp, then nearly dropped the knife in her attempt to cut into it.

"Careful. Don't hurt yourself." Levi's deep tone rumbled next to her.

Annie turned to give him what for, but her stinging retort died on her lips at the deliberate mocking gleam in his eye. He was baiting her. Well, this was one fish he would not catch.

# Chapter Three

How in the heck could this be happening? It was one thing to sit next to a spoiled, daddy's girl through dinner, but to be her escort for an entire weekend was something else. Levi jabbed his salad, wracking his brain for some way to get out of it but knew, even as he did so, it would not only be impossible, but rude for him to suggest it to Mark.

Liddy, Lord bless her, had assured him he would just love *her Annie*. At the time, he'd smiled indulgently at Liddy's attempt at matchmaking, but this girl held absolutely no interest for him. *So why can't you shake those amazing brown eyes of hers?* He adjusted his shirt collar, which suddenly took on suffocating proportion.

And what was this *Dell* business. Her name was Delany. He eyed her, curiosity and police training taking on mega proportions. He made a mental note to check out that little discrepancy at the station.

But in the meantime, he couldn't very well suggest Liddy get another maid of honor. He'd just have to play his part. Try to be on his best behavior. *Try* to be a gentleman. He stabbed at a clump of lettuce, then a tomato wedge, and stuffed both in his mouth.

He cut his eyes in Annie's direction. A rigid ice queen. Eyes downcast, she played with her food, pushing a pink shrimp around her plate like a hockey puck.

"You're supposed to eat it, not play with it."

"Excuse me?" Golden, battle-ready brown eyes glistened up at him.

"Your salad. Don't you like it?"

"Don't bother with small talk. Let's just get through this," she whispered vehemently. When she pursed her lips, they took on the shape of a small, pink flower. The sudden urge to kiss those delectable lips pummeled his brain. He sucked in a slow, steadying breath.

"Pouting?" He raised a brow in her direction. "It figures. Another admirable trait of a *daddy's girl.*"

Annie spun toward him. Her formerly pursed, pink lips parted in surprise, bringing a twinge of guilt to his conscience. Her eyes clouded over and for a millisecond a slight, pained expression crossed her face. He hadn't thought of her as being overly sensitive. Of course he knew nothing about her and if he wasn't careful, he might say something he'd later regret. Dread settled in his gut at the weekend that loomed in front of him.

The sudden flash of her golden eyes brought him out of his reverie.

"You can give me a ticket for speeding and for using my cell phone, but you have no right to tell me when and what I should eat."

"Contrary, too." He shook his head just like he did when handing out tickets to irresponsible, non-thinking civilians "Now why am I not surprised?"

Annie pushed herself away from the table with such force she almost fell backward. His arm shot out to steady her chair. At her sharp inhale, his eyes locked with hers. In one heart stopping moment he watched her creamy cheeks flush to a delicate pink before she jumped from her seat. Blue chiffon spilled from her waist to just below her knees, swishing along her slender legs as she hurried from the room.

* * *

Annie pushed through the bathroom door, snatched up a tissue, then took refuge in one of the stalls. She stood in the four by six cubical and dabbed her eyes. That *daddy's girl* comment really grated. She was anything but. She sniffed. So, she'd tried to talk her way out of a ticket. Was that a crime? She thought about her behavior after he'd pulled her over and cringed. Part of her couldn't blame him for thinking so poorly of her. And so what if he'd called her a daddy's girl. She needed to shake it off. Besides, it wasn't like she wasn't used to being labeled, especially since Alex's arrest.

Oh, why did she have to get up and run? That's all she seemed to be good for lately. Fleeing her home for a better future in New York. Fleeing the news media and the unfair accusations she heard daily on radio and TV. And most recently, running off to the hotel bathroom to escape…

What? A two bit, insignificant, small town sheriff?

A big fish in a very little pond?

Sure, he was gorgeous to look at, but as far as she was concerned that was the extent of it. Taking a deep cleansing yoga breath, she sucked it up and made her way back to the table.

Liddy had told her about Mark's best man as if he were some knight in shining armor. Had built him up so much that Annie couldn't wait to meet him. She'd come to believe that he must be pretty wonderful and had actually looked forward to spending the weekend as his date.

But, he was just like everyone else. Saw only what was on the outside. Another male ego throwing his masculine weight around. Well, she was through with all that. She had escaped it once and swore she'd never be bullied again.

* * *

*Bully sheriff.* Levi had been called that on more than one occasion. Hatefully by some and endearingly by others. Well, if that's what it took to keep little misses like her alive, so be it. But, this was the first time he'd ever caused a woman to literally get up and run. Guilt rose and shook its ugly, accusatory finger in his face. Trying his best to ignore it, he jabbed his fork into the fleshy shrimp, nearly cracking the plate.

"What's wrong with Annie?" Liddy swiveled in her seat and looked right at him. "Did you say something to her?"

If the accusatory darts in her eyes were bullets, he'd be a dead man.

He raised his hands in surrender. "Not a thing."

"Sure you didn't."

Liddy's eyes lit up with something in between mischief and accusation, reminding him of the snapping turtle he'd had to get out of Mrs. Radcliff's swimming pool.

"Don't tell me. Did the *bully sheriff* act again?" she asked.

He gazed down at her heart-shaped face and tried not to smile. She did look like Mrs. Radcliff's snapping turtle. A cute one, but nevertheless, Mark was certainly going to have his hands full.

"I think Miss *Dell* is perfectly capable of taking care of herself." He waited, hoping Liddy would clear up the Dell-Delany mystery, but she didn't.

"Honestly, Levi, you'll never find a woman, treating them like you do. One would think you had no interest in settling down and having a family. And that constant scowl on your face has got to go, if only for the weekend."

"Believe it or not, I don't need your help in the dating department. I'm fully capable of finding my own wife. And my scowl stays put, young lady. I like it that way." He winked.

"Oh, please. Annie is perfect for you. I just know it. Besides, you need to learn to listen to me, as your future best friend-in-law."

"Oh, so that's what this is about. You just want Annie to be *your* best friend-in-law, as well. One big happy family, right?"

"Hey, am I going to have to separate you two?" Mark teased.

"It's your soon-to-be mouthy bride that's causing all the trouble. If you'd rein her in occasionally—"

"Oh, don't think I haven't thought about it." Mark said, eyes twinkling.

"Hey!" Liddy smacked Mark good and hard, which had Mark grabbing his arm then buckling over to feign injury.

"Or, I could arrest her for you." Levi grinned over at Mark. "A couple of nights in jail should tame her. You sure you want to marry this termagant?"

Liddy folded her arms across her chest and rolled her blue eyes.

"Hey, find your own woman to tame and leave mine to me." Mark wrapped his arm around Liddy's waist, pulled her to his side, and kissed her neck.

"Okay, you two. You've had your fun." Liddy pushed away from Mark, then rested her hand on Levi's arm.

He gazed down at her upturned face. All joking aside, he was truly happy for Mark, who was closer to a brother in more ways than he could count.

"So, what do you think of her? Isn't she gorgeous?" Liddy gushed.

"Ah, yeah. She's a looker all right." As soon as he spoke he wished he'd answered her differently. The dagger look was back on Liddy's face and told him in no uncertain terms that he now had some explaining to do.

"A looker? Are you kidding me?" Her small fists snapped at her waist. "What is up with you?" Her eyes widened. "You did say something to her. I swear, Levi, if you've upset her—"

"All right, you might as well know" He was never one to mince words. "I find your friend a spoiled daddy's girl."

"You couldn't be more wrong about her."

"I'm afraid your friendship has blinded you, little one, and I may as well tell you now before you hear her version. I gave her two tickets earlier today."

"That was you?" Liddy's eyes danced with laughter.

Not the reaction he was expecting.

"Buddy, you deserve whatever you get this weekend." She raised her finger and shook it in his face. "And it'll happen when you least expect it."

"What is that supposed to mean?" He was suddenly wary. But could say no more as the object of their discussion reappeared.

"You okay?" Liddy asked as Annie took her seat.

"Perfectly," Annie responded with a bright, engaging smile, which she turned on him at that moment. Unprepared for the onslaught to his senses, the coy, sparkle-eyed female now sitting next to him was close to unrecognizable. But when she dropped her eyes shyly to her plate, he could have sworn he spotted a small smile of victory pass her lips.

* * *

Maybe it was being was away from New York and in this cocoon of a town that made her regain some of her spunk and energy. She wasn't sure, but suddenly she was ready to teach someone a lesson. And right now, that someone was sitting right next to her and she couldn't think of anyone more deserving of a lesson than him.

She'd have to sneak into it, though. Couldn't just come across as someone completely different than who she'd been up to that point. She'd have to slow dance into it. A light bulb flickered in her head. That's it. There would be dancing tonight and he would have to ask her. It would look odd if he didn't. Especially after what Liddy had told her about him. *A real gentleman, tough as nails at times, but only when he had to be.* Some gentleman. She had yet to see it.

Mark and Liddy got up to dance, giving Annie her opening. She deliberately dropped her fork on the floor near his chair, then gave him the barest of moments to retrieve it before leaning down herself to pick it up. At this angle, she was certain he'd have a nice, clear view down the top of her dress. As she suspected, he quickly grabbed it off the floor and, after a brief glance at her chest stood to his feet.

"I'll get you another."

That was easy. Placing her hands primly in her lap, she waited for him to return. He was back in no time and handed her a clean fork.

"Thank you."

"You're welcome."

"This lemon pepper sauce is delicious, isn't it?" She gave him a brief smile. Her heart clattered in her chest at the bold, assessing look he gave her. *Easy does it, girl. He's already thinking something isn't right, here.* She cut into the chicken and took another bite.

She swallowed. "You know, I can't help but think we got off on the wrong foot earlier today."

"You mean your lead foot?" He spread butter on a piece of crusty bread.

She bristled, but covered it by saying in her sweetest voice, "Yes, my big, fat lead foot. Which certainly has gotten in the way of what I was hoping would be a lovely weekend. I've heard so many nice things about you from Liddy. Can't we just pretend today didn't happen?"

She watched him closely for his reaction. It had better be a favorable one because it galled her to no earthly end to have to gush all over him like that. She kept her most lovely sincere smile on her face as she waited for his response.

*Come on. Come on.*

Yeeessss. Good. Here it comes…the subtle twinkle in his eyes, the slight crook of his lips, revealing at last the smile she knew was in that stoic face of his.

Victory. Sweet as the chocolate mousse the server was setting before her.

"Ooo, this looks great." Annie dove into the rich, decadent, dessert. Pleased with her success thus far, she deliberately licked the chocolate from her spoon.

"Liddy tells me you're a model."

Annie dabbed her lips with the silver edged napkin. "Yes, I am."

"What kind of modeling?"

"Standard run of the mill stuff. Fashion—"

"You mean like those flyers from the Sunday newspapers?"

She glanced up at him, thinking he was joking. But his eyes held what seemed to be an honest forthright enquiry. He wasn't kidding. She knew she was looking at him like he was crazy, but she couldn't help it. Light finally dawned. He didn't know who she was. Even after pulling her over and reading her name on her license, he didn't know. Could this night get any better?

"No, nothing like that," she said.

"Then like what, Sears?" His expression was guileless.

"Not in a long time. Now, I mainly model the high end stuff, both runway and print, of course."

"Print?"

"Yes. I've done numerous spreads in *Vogue*, *Cosmopolitan*, *Glamour*, and *Marie Claire*. *Elle*."

"But not Sears."

"No."

"What's wrong with Sears?"

"Nothing's wrong with Sears. I got my start with Sears. They—"

His eyes held a definitive gleam in their depths.

*He was toying with her!*

She clamped her mouth shut and turned her back on him, but not before she heard his low chuckle.

Fine, considering her afternoon's performance, she guessed she deserved that.

The dessert plates were cleared away, the servers topped off the wine glasses, then stepped aside.

Annie took a sip of Sauvignon Blanc and glanced at Levi. He had shoved his chair back from the table and sat holding his wine glass in his right hand while perusing her with his keen baby blues.

Blatantly.

Openly.

Audaciously.

Fine, she could handle his rude stares. She'd been ogled by far worse than him. She tilted her head to one side and smiled. The smile photographer Dave Mandel of

*Glamour Magazine* claimed was irresistible. Well, no time like the present to put that ridiculous statement to the test.

"So, Sheriff." She scooted her chair closer to his and the sudden alarm that entered his eyes was delicious. She lifted her glass in the air. "I propose we call a truce. After all, we're here to celebrate the wedding of your best friend and my best friend. And since we've been paired for the weekend, by the matchmaking bride, we may as well make the most of it."

She gave him her most candid, but coy expression, daring him to disagree. "What do you say?" she coaxed softly.

"How could I deny such an earnest and sincere request?"

Something about the way he said it churned her insides, but she gave nothing away as she smiled brightly at him. Tilting his head in salute, he raised his glass and touched it to hers, the sound of crystal sealing the deal.

# Chapter Four

Levi casually sipped his wine, and watched her. He hadn't missed the slight flush to her cheeks when he'd raised his glass to hers. If anything, it made her more beautiful. Gave her an innocence he was certain she didn't possess. The small orchestra began to play and several more couples moved to the dance floor.

"Would you like to dance?" he asked.

She lifted her eyes to his and blinked. Pleased to see he had surprised her, he stood and held out his hand.

*I'm not the small town bumpkin you thought I was.*

She hesitated, but only for a moment, then stood and placed her hand in his. He led her to the dance floor and deftly took her into his arms. He placed his hand against the small of her back and pulled her closer. Her silky dress did little to hide her slender form or the warmth emanating from her skin. He couldn't lie. The combination of chiffon and flesh raised his heart up a notch. Her lips parted and she drew in a deep breath. The small, but audible sound pleased him. Could he actually be making little miss snooty nervous? Her chest rose and fell as she strove to gain her footing. "Sorry, is my grip too tight?"

"No. No, it's fine."

She was lying. He was trained to know when someone wasn't telling him the truth.

"You dance beautifully," she said.

"You sound surprised."

"I am. In New York, I went dancing often. You'd be surprised how few men can dance. Really well, I mean. Most of them have two left feet and by the end of the evening my toes would end up black and blue."

Open and frank, her eyes held just a hint of laughter. His stomach lurched at her candid, forthright gaze. Wholesome. That he wasn't expecting and he was surprised at the sudden pull against his ribs. He didn't much like it. He liked it better when she played it coy. That he could deal with. This sudden, sweet innocent act was just that, an act. He deliberately twirled her hard and fast around another couple. She gasped, nearly losing her footing. Daggers shot from her eyes.

*There she is.* She couldn't stand him. Well, that was fine with him. The feeling was mutual.

"So, Sears gave you your start."

She raised honey brown eyes to his and nodded. "I was thirteen."

"Thirteen? Isn't that a bit young to start painting your face and wearing clothes many adult women won't even wear?"

"You obviously don't know anything about thirteen-year-old girls. They're on the brink. Soon to blossom. Their self-images, delicate. Please tell me you don't have a thirteen-year-old daughter, because if you do, I'm sure an intervention would be in order."

"And I'm *sure* in some circles your opinion is without fault, but you're in the south, lady, and a small town. We do things differently down here."

"Well, do you?"

"Do I what?"

"Have a thirteen-year-old daughter?"

He grinned. "What do you think?"

"Well, that all depends. How do you do that down here in the south?"

He tried to still the laughter, but couldn't. The look on her face alone, when she realized what she said, would be worth the entire weekend with her. "I imagine we *do that* the same way you *do it* up north," he said.

"That's not what I meant," she hissed. "Your mind is in the gutter."

"The gutter? Is that what you call it up north?" He delighted in her smoldering brown eyes and her discomfort. "Here, we call it ecstasy."

* * *

The Florida sunshine fell through the crack in the blinds, spilling across Annie's face. She squinted against the bright light, turned to her side, and placed her hands under her cheek. After she and Levi had ended their dance, she'd quickly said good night and stomped off. So what if she'd left him standing in the middle of the dance floor. He'd been impossible and had made fun of her all evening.

*And I guess you haven't had similar motives toward him since he pulled you over?* She hated it when her sensible self admonished her.

She rolled onto her back and sighed. When Liddy had shared her plans for her wedding party, Annie had so looked forward to them—before she'd met Levi Hawke, that is. But the delicious thought of teaching Robo Cop a lesson had her jumping from the bed to get dressed.

This morning, after breakfast, they were all going to the beach. As Annie pulled her kelly-green one-piece bathing suit from her suitcase, she wished now she'd brought a bikini instead. This one-piece fit her beautifully, but if she was to snag the sheriff, she needed something a bit more revealing. She pursed her lips. This would have to do.

She made her way downstairs to the sunny dining room. A pretty blonde hostess led her to a small table near the entrance.

"Coffee?" she asked while pouring Annie a glass of fresh squeezed orange juice.

"Yes, please."

Not much of a big breakfast eater, Annie ordered one egg over easy and a bagel, then settled back to enjoy her coffee. As she sipped the hot liquid, she spied a small boutique across the way and made a mental note to check it out after breakfast.

Eddie and Kathie Cummings walked by the entrance and waved to her.

"You're coming to the beach this morning, aren't you?" Kathie asked.

"Absolutely. I'm just getting a bit of a late start. Where do we go? Is it close?"

"Yes, it's just outside. You'll see the path through the sand dunes. It leads right to the beach."

"Wonderful. I'll see you guys soon," Annie said.

After breakfast, Annie put the bill on her room and walked over to the boutique. It was filled with an array of seashells, costume jewelry, colorful cover-ups, and a nice selection of bathing suits. Her eyes immediately fell on a pretty lavender string bikini. Small green paisleys dotted the lilac fabric with their signature curls. She lifted it off the rack to check the size, then stepped into the booth to try it on. It was perfect. It should work magic on the sheriff.

"If it doesn't, he's not human."

After slipping on her cover-up, Annie paid with her VISA. It was time she joined the party or Liddy would be wondering where she was.

* * *

Levi finished his morning run just as Annie strolled onto the beach. She was wearing white polka dot sunglasses and a wide-brimmed straw hat. A white cover-up clung to her in all the right places, with slits up the sides revealing her long, slender legs. He paused and stared. There was something about her that seemed familiar. But that was impossible because until yesterday, he'd never met her before.

Last night, after she'd left him standing on the dance floor, he'd vowed to ignore her the rest of the weekend. But one look at her long limbs, now picture perfect on the blue lounger, had him rethinking that vow. If he didn't know better he'd swear she was posing for one of those photo shoots she'd talked about.

Wait. That was it. He must have seen her in an ad or something. The way she leaned back in the chair, head tilted to one side, looking out to sea. He'd seen that very image before.

She was quite beautiful, a knockout. She lowered her sunglasses and peeked at him over the top of the frames. Then raised her hot-pink nail-polished fingers in the air and gave him a feminine wave. The slight smile that curved her satiny lips was difficult to ignore. He nodded to her, then could have kicked himself. Was he that soft? He clenched his jaw and strode to the water's edge. He dove in at a safe depth and swam away from the shore-line.

The cool salt water flowed over his sweaty flesh like silk. He needed to cool down in more ways than one.

He'd participated in IRONMAN Florida last year and was still in the best shape of his life. His powerful strokes could take him as far away from the shore as he pleased, but it would seem odd to Mark and Liddy if he didn't re-turn soon. Stopping to tread water, he thought of his sis-ter. This week marked ten years since she'd been killed. Another reason he was acting like a wounded bear. Over the past several years, he'd done a pretty good job mask-ing his emotions, until Annie Dell showed up knocking his well-placed façade completely off kilter.

He came out of the water and shook his head, then ran his fingers through his hair. He approached the blue umbrellas and matching sling chairs that identified the wedding party, careful not to give Annie a single glance. As he reached for his beach towel, he could see she was watching him. *Fine, let her look.* And she could keep on looking, because that's all she'd get from him this weekend. He was no pawn in anyone's game, especially that of a spoiled New York socialite. Did she really think he was such a fool not to recognize when someone was toying with him? It was obvious she had never lived in the real world. A world where life wasn't perfect, where people have real needs and suffer hurts and daily disappointments. Annie Dell needed some real world lessons.

"I wondered if you were ever coming back." Mark handed him a cold bottle of water.

Levi took a long swig and sat back in the lounger. "I wondered the same thing."

"You okay?" Mark said.

"Yes." He glanced at Mark and crooked a smile. "Your concern is appreciated, but not necessary."

"When Liddy and I chose this date we didn't realize it fell on the same week as Karen's death. I'm sorry, man."

"No reason to be."

Mark nodded toward the water. "The last time I saw you swim like that when it wasn't a race was—"

"Hey, drop it."

Mark sighed. "It's been ten years. You can't keep blaming yourself. She wouldn't want you to."

Needing something to do in that moment, Levi slapped the towel against his sand encrusted feet. He glanced at Mark's pensive face and was immediately sorry for his earlier reaction. "I know. I didn't mean to bite your head off. But it's hard not to blame myself when it was my fault."

"It was the driver's fault."

"Don't think I haven't told myself that a thousand times." He settled back in the chair. "If I'd been doing my job, it wouldn't have happened."

"Don't say that." Mark clasped Levi's shoulder. "I'm sorry I brought it up, but you've got something on your mind. What is it?"

Levi glanced over at Mark whose raised brow and intense stare signaled this conversation wasn't over.

He shook his head, knowing he couldn't pull anything over on Mark. "It's nothing I can't handle."

"Well that's certainly gotten my attention. What's going on, Sheriff? Sounds like somebody could be in trouble?"

"It's your wedding weekend. You really don't want to know."

"Uh, oh. That sounds too close to home." He grinned. "Please tell me it's not my adorable, trouble-making bride."

Levi stared out over the water. "Don't worry. It's nothing to do with you or Liddy."

"Don't worry, he says. You forget. I've seen that look before. I know you. Once you get an idea about something, *or* someone, you're like a pit bull. Like you said, this is my wedding weekend. So, whatever it is, just let it go."

"How much do you know about Annie?" Levi asked. She was chatting with Liddy and Beth. They had their heads together and were laughing about something. Compared to the other two, Annie sparkled. He clenched his jaw and glanced back at Mark.

"Oh, so that's it." Mark grinned. "She got to you, too?"

"What do you mean, too?"

"You mean as an officer of the law you haven't noticed?"

"Noticed what, damn it?"

Mark chuckled. "Macon. He hasn't been able to keep his eyes off her since he met her."

Levi glanced back at the women. Kathie had pulled up a chair and joined them. He looked over at Eddie and Macon, who were sitting nearby. Eddie was talking and looking out over the water, but Macon was clearly not paying attention to whatever Eddie was saying. He was eyeing the group of women, obviously focused on Annie. Good Lord, he looked like an adoring puppy.

He could hardly stand to watch and turned his attention back to Mark, who was visibly amused.

"You see?" Mark asked.

"Buddy, he can have her."

Mark burst out laughing.

"What in blazes is so funny?"

"You." Mark shook his head. "How the mighty has fallen."

# Chapter Five

Annie was never more aware of anyone in her life. When she joined the group, she was certain she'd gotten Levi's attention, but to be completely ignored by anyone she'd set her sights on was a bit unusual. Of course, in this case, her *sights* had nothing to do with romance and everything to do with teaching Robo Cop a lesson.

She'd had to learn about men much sooner than she should have. When she arrived in New York, very young and green, she quickly learned that she had fled from one kind of danger only to be thrust into another. Most men weren't like her father, but that didn't mean they were saints either.

There were photographers who expected payback for publishing her in fine magazines. Male models who stared at her across the changing room during fashion shows. Until, one day, salvation came in the form of a small energetic woman named Liz Conners. She'd come backstage after a show and asked to represent Annie. That was the day her life changed. Liz was honest and reputable in the talent and modeling business. A God-send if there ever was one. She found Annie a safe hostel in which to live, even encouraged her to finish high school. She taught Annie the ropes of the industry and found her a financial advisor to help her save and invest for her future.

But men still wanted her, and let her know it. That's when she made the deal with Alex. They'd met through one of her charity events and he seemed a kind and thoughtful man. Since women were after him, mainly for his money, he suggested a plan that would serve them both. He would have a beautiful escort to all of the hottest society functions and she would have his protection. Handsome and confident and with his financial background, he'd won her over. It was a win-win. Or so she'd thought.

Annie pulled herself out of her muse.

"Chips?" Beth Turner was holding out a bowl toward her.

"Oh, no. But thanks." Annie placed a hand to her mid-section. "I just ate." She glanced over at Levi. He was sitting in one of the blue canvas chairs talking with

Mark. Tanned and fit, he embodied the perfect picture of outdoorsman and athlete. North Face to her Prada.

She sighed. This was not going well. He was certainly doing a good job of ignoring her. At this rate the wedding would be over and he would be back to his officer duties before she could put him in his *place* once and for all. His sudden glance in her direction gave her a start. His blue eyes bore into hers and she had this uncanny feeling that he knew what she was up to. Knew what she'd been thinking. After all, he was an officer of the law. They were trained to know these things. She pulled on her bottom lip and looked away.

"Excuse me, ladies. I think I'll take a walk." *It's show time.*

"Okay." Beth and Kathie spoke at the same time.

"Don't get sunburned." Liddy's voice held a warning. "Remember my wedding's tomorrow."

Annie rolled her eyes, stood, and casually let her cover-up drop to the chair. She stifled a giggle at Liddy's wide-eyed stare. After giving her friend a sisterly wink, she strolled past Mark and Levi.

"Good morning, guys." Their conversation came to a screeching halt and she gave them a sunny smile. As she passed Levi's chair, she deliberately raised her arms to adjust the wide brimmed hat perched on her head, then caught the look on Levi's face. Icy blue chips followed her. If eyes could talk, his were spewing curses about now. At least it was nice to know she could get to him.

The gulf water foamed, warm and sensual over her bare feet. The sugar white sand squished pleasantly between her toes. She loved the push and pull of the water around her ankles. The ocean had a life of its own. Strong and powerful. Taking hold and commanding anyone or anything that crossed its path. Like some men. And, one in particular. A raw ache shot through her heart. She swallowed hard. Now why was she thinking about him? She'd blocked him out for years and only rarely did he ever enter her thoughts. Until something triggered it. She shivered. If she'd had that kind of power she'd never use it to hurt anyone, especially a child.

Spotting a sand dollar near her feet, she stopped at the water's edge. Delighted, she bent down and picked it up. She turned the treasure over in her hands and ran her fingers gently over its surface. The five-leafed flower in the center was beautiful in its simplicity.

"Careful. They're very delicate."

Annie spun around at the sound of Levi's deep voice.

"The least amount of pressure and they can break to pieces."

She gazed up at him and caught her breath. He stood inches from her and seemed so much taller. Without his uniform, all bare-chested and brown, he was a compelling figure. Vibrant blue eyes crinkled against the glare as he stood looking down at her. Or, was it through her. She was wearing sunglasses and a straw hat but somehow it was she who felt exposed.

"I've never found a sand dollar before. It's beautiful."

"There're several types. This one is the Key Hole Sand Dollar." He pointed to the middle hole in the front. "See?"

"Right. It looks like it would fit one of those old fashion keys." She turned it over in her hand. "I can't believe it didn't break. How something can be so delicate and yet able to survive the pounding of the waves is amazing. It must be stronger than we think."

"It's in its element," he said.

She tilted her head to look at him. He was eyeing her as if he wasn't sure about something. She shook it off and smiled. "Thank you for sharing that."

He nodded.

"So. I see you decided to take a walk," she said. "Or, were you just following me?"

He squinted out over the ocean, then gazed back down at her. "I think we both know I didn't *just* take a walk."

Annie pressed the sand dollar to her chest.

"Careful. You'll crush it." He gently removed it from her clutch. "Here. Hold it like this." His fingers brushed her palm as he placed the sand dollar, almost reverently, in her hand.

Riveted, she watched him, surprised by his gentle touch. His arm encircled her waist and in one smooth motion, pulled her to him. Coppertone and sea salt filled her senses. She flattened her free hand against his chest and held her breath.

Warmth simmered between them and it wasn't the mid-morning sun. She stood still and waited for his kiss. When his eyes locked with hers, everything around her faded into insignificance, the waves, the sun, the sky. It all melted away, leaving only him.

He brought his hand to her face and ran his fingers down her cheek. Her skin tingled with expectation.

"I think we both know the dangers of playing with matches," he said.

She blinked, his words bringing her back to awareness.

"Brush fires can be quite difficult to put out." He cupped her chin and gazed deeply into her eyes. "They spread so quickly."

She stepped away, and he dropped his hand to his side.

"Afraid?" He cocked an arrogant brow in her direction.

"I think we'd better get back." She licked her suddenly dry lips. "The others will be wondering where we are."

"I highly doubt it. But if you say so." It was evident in his sparkling blue eyes and the slight tilt of his lips that he was enjoying himself.

They started back down the shore to the others. Periodically she stole a glance in his direction and caught him looking at her with that candid expression from the night before. After the third time she thought it best to keep looking straight ahead.

No doubt, he was playing with her nerves. She was reminded of the day he'd trailed behind her in his patrol car. Like a watchful hawk, talons flared, before the kill. She shivered.

"Cold or has someone walked over your grave?" His gleaming eyes, coupled with that devastatingly handsome tilt of his lips was enough to set off a dozen fire alarms. *Now who's playing with matches?*

"Neither." She shrugged. "I was just thinking of something."

"Care to share?"

Annie chose not to answer. No use giving him any ammunition he could use on her later.

* * *

Mark and Liddy's wedding was straight out of a fairy tale. Liddy's pearl laden dress shimmered as she walked alongside her father down the boardwalk. With the ocean spanning the foreground, Mark and Liddy were married on the pristine beaches of Apalacha Key. The warm and informal ceremony was officiated by their pastor who promised many blessings for the happy couple. When it was over, the late afternoon sunlight bathed the bride and groom as they walked back down the makeshift aisle as Mr. and Mrs. Mark Allen Carmichael.

The reception was held back at the hotel's small ballroom. Wedding guests were already in line to partake of the simple buffet dinner of roast beef, rosemary potatoes, and steamed vegetables. To the left an ice sculpture adorned a table laden with fresh boiled shrimp and to the right, oysters on the half shell. A white frothy three-tiered cake stood in the opposite corner of the room, with a small decadent chocolate groom's cake next to it.

The joyous occasion culminated with eloquent toasts from the best man and the maid of honor followed by the bride and groom's first dance as a married couple.

Before Mark and Liddy were to leave, Liddy pulled Annie close. "Have fun the rest of the evening and don't be too hard on Levi. Mark says there is a reason he's the way he is and that he doesn't like to talk about it."

"I bet he doesn't."

"Don't you dare say anything to him about what I just told you. Mark swore me to secrecy."

"Not a great way to start your marriage, kiddo."

"You're my best friend. That's what best friends are for - telling and keeping secrets." Liddy's eyes held a mischievous twinkle. "By the way, everything at the house is ready for your mini escape. I have some staples in the fridge, but you'll have to go grocery shopping for anything else you want. The car rental company will pick up your car tomorrow. You can use mine while I'm gone."

"What about the teenage girls I'm supposed to work with after my Miami shoot?"

"It's all set. The principal of the high school, Amanda Marsh, is expecting your call. She has everything set up for you."

"Listen." Annie took hold of Liddy's hands. "You guys are great to let me stay in your new home. I'm so sick of hotels. I can't thank you enough."

"Wait until you see the boxes that are still stacked everywhere before you go thanking me." Liddy squeezed Annie's hands. "I wish I could have had everything unpacked for you."

"No worries. It'll give me something to do. I'm happy to finish up the unpacking."

"You will not." Liddy tugged sharply on Annie's hands. "You're here to relax."

"Fine." Annie laughed. "I'll just hang a few pictures."

"Decorate to your heart's content, but promise me you'll relax and take care of yourself. After what you've been through you deserve it. Are you sure you're going to be okay?"

"Yes." Annie gave Liddy a quick hug. "Having this time out of the limelight will be heavenly."

"You've lost too much weight, too. I expect to see you fattened up when I get back." Liddy continued as if Annie hadn't spoken. "I know models are supposed to be thin but, really?"

Annie touched her forehead to Liddy's. "Quit worrying," she playfully admonished. "It's your wedding day and you're about to leave on your honeymoon with the love of your life."

"I am aren't I?" Liddy sighed happily.

"Yes, you are."

"Someday it'll be your turn. You'll see."

Annie smiled at her naïve friend. Life wasn't a fairy tale but no need to spoil it for her. Liddy would have her trials soon enough.

The newlyweds ran through the cascades of white rice to the open door of the black limousine, ducked into the low opening, then were gone. Just like that, months of planning came to an end. Annie sighed and gazed after them and thought about Liddy's parting words, 'someday, it'll be your turn.' She wished she could believe it, but knew from experience that knights in shining armor didn't exist.

# Chapter Six

Annie turned and collided smack into Levi, who was standing right behind her. He steadied her with a pair of strong hands causing her skin to tingle delightfully. She sucked in her breath and gazed up at him.

"Excuse me, I didn't realize you were there," she said.

Dressed in a black tux he was certainly one of the most outstanding male specimens she'd ever seen. And, in her line of business, that was saying something. Too bad what was underneath was such a hard-unbreakable shell. For two days she'd tried all of her feminine wiles on him but seemingly to no avail. Except for that moment on the beach when he pulled her to him and she'd panicked. Well, next time she wouldn't. She so wanted to put him in his place after what he'd said to her.

"Well, I'd say that came off without too much of a hitch, wouldn't you?"

"Yes, it was a beautiful wedding." They turned in unison to walk back inside. The orchestra was still playing and the night still young, but part of her just wanted to leave. Not that she didn't enjoy the beautiful life, she'd experienced it long enough, but the past weeks of trying to avoid photographers and the media, then keeping up appearances at Liddy's wedding was beginning to take its toll.

But, she wouldn't call it a night before this *daddy's girl*, dealt with Robo Cop. She gave her escort a sideways glance. The underlying smirk that took residence on his handsome face galled her and compelled her to try one last idea.

"I thought you made a very nice toast tonight. What you said about Mark…a man that is not afraid to live life to the fullest and…" Annie hesitated, looking to him for the rest.

"And embrace what is truly important," he finished.

She nodded. "Very nice."

"It wasn't hard. Mark and I are more like brothers than anything else."

"I know."

"And what about you and Liddy? I understand you two have quite a history."

"We do, yes. She and I were childhood friends. After she and her family moved to Florida, we'd spend weeks together in the summers. It was wonderful. A haven for me."

"Really? In what way?"

She shrugged. "Stability for one. My father and I moved around a lot. Finally settling in Iowa. That's where I met Liddy."

She glanced up at his face. He was looking at her with a pensive expression. As if he was trying to figure something out.

"Would you like to dance?" he asked.

She licked her kips and continued to stare at him. His expression had softened. He seemed less perplexed about her. Hard to tell if he was testing her or if he was being genuine.

"I'd love to." Actually, she didn't want to do anything with him, but teach him a lesson. That 'spoiled daddy's girl' comment still stung and the last place she wanted to be was in his arms. But when he slid them around her waist, her legs went all weak and wobbly and it wasn't from being in high heels for the past four hours.

Levi pulled her close, maneuvering her expertly around the marble floor in a waltz. She caught her breath at his perfect, smooth execution of the steps, twirling her like a gentleman from a Regency romance novel. A shimmy ran up her spine. When they came to a stop, she was breathless and could only look up at him in wonder.

"Where did you learn to dance like that?"

"I'd like to say it was the annual policeman's ball, but my mother had a dancing school."

He smiled down at her with a warm light in his eyes. Something thudded in her chest and her heart skipped a beat.

"Policeman's ball. But, you're a sheriff."

"I used to be a cop."

She watched him close up. Just like that, the light had gone out.

He placed his hand at the small of her back and led her off the floor back to their table.

"I see from the signs around town that you're running for re-election this fall."

"That's right." His voice sounded aloof and disinterested.

So, he was back to being his cool self. Talk about washing hot then cold.

*Whatever.*

She pursed her lips. She knew her fixation to get back at him was probably bordering on obsession but she didn't care. She'd give it one final push. If he didn't take the bait, she'd forget this whole revenge thing.

"Well, I'm done in, I'm afraid. Thank you for the dance." She spun away and strolled back to their table.

"This is early for someone like you, isn't it? I would have thought staying up all hours was more your style."

If he weren't the sheriff, she'd have landed him a facer right then and there. Instead, she gave him her sweetest smile. "For an officer of the law, I'm surprised you give in so quickly to…preconceived notions."

His firm mouth lifted at the corners. "Let's see. You're a high fashion model, you enjoy nightclubs and dancing. You're an incorrigible flirt and have been after me all weekend. Have I missed something?"

A warm flush crept up her neck. "What ever happened to innocent until proven guilty?" She waited a second for that to sink in.

"I get the impression you're hiding something." He shrugged. "Makes me wonder if you *are* guilty."

Her heart raced at the expression on his face. What was it with him? Why did he like to taunt her? Why did he dislike her?

"Yea, I'm guilty. As charged." She held out her hands. "Would you like to haul me in? Torture a confession out of me?"

"That won't be necessary." Amusement lit his eyes. "But I'll walk you to your room."

*Of course you will. Proving you're nothing but a man after all. Who only thinks of one thing.*

"Why, thank you, Sheriff." She coyly batted her eyes to add to the fun.

He grinned. Wolf like. And her heart slammed into her stomach. "Shall we go?" She swallowed against the sudden attack of nerves, hoping the lump in her throat would ease up a bit.

He waved his arm toward the bank of elevators that sat near the entrance to the ballroom.

"After you."

When the elevator door closed, Annie pressed the number four button. Deafening silence filled the space. Both of them stood like statues staring upward as the single digits clicked by. One, two, three, finally stopping at four. The doors opened, and Annie stepped out. Levi followed close behind.

"My room is just down this way." She had to break the silence that fell between them. Awkward would not get her the result she wanted. Best to keep things running smoothly.

Annie pulled the key card from her purse and slid it in the lock. At the green light and single click she pushed open her door and went inside. She turned toward him, catching her bottom lip between her teeth and giving him the 'come hither' look she used when modeling lingerie.

Levi looked from right to left then stepped into her doorway. He pushed the door to, but didn't completely shut it. That worked for her, as she wasn't planning on having him stay very long.

Heart thudding, she stepped closer, and without a word pulled his bow tie free of his collar. She tossed it aside, then began unbuttoning his shirt, which proved a bit more difficult. Her fingers fumbled beside the top button under his chin. The crisp, starchy fabric stuck to her thumbs. Levi shoved her hand aside and undid it for her.

She placed one hand around the back of his head and pulled him to her. She brushed her lips along his firm mouth, giving him one feathery kiss. "Patience, Sheriff." She forced a seductive smile, while her heart hammered in her chest. "I'll get there."

She placed her fingers on the next button. Still stiff, but she managed well enough. When she reached the middle of his chest she glanced at him. Her hands stilled. She caught her breath. His smoldering blue eyes glistened, suddenly making it difficult for her to breathe. She hesitated not quite sure she should continue. After all, he could be dangerous…for all she knew he could—

"Keep going."

He spoke with such quiet authority that her fingers obeyed. She grasped the white fabric and pulled the shirt tail from the confines of his trousers. When she unclasped the last button she glanced back up. His blue eyes challenged, beckoned, and dared all at the same time. But there was something else. She couldn't quite put her finger on what it was, but it was most certainly there. Then it hit her. He knew. Knew exactly what she was up to.

So. He thought she was the mouse to his cat did he? Well, he'd soon see. Never one to ignore a dare, she took a deep breath and summoned every ounce of courage at her disposal. Reaching up, she peeled the dress shirt from his shoulders until it, too, was on the floor.

The white undershirt fit Levi like a second skin.

"Allow me." He pulled it up and over his head in seconds. Oakmoss and Cedarwood filtered through the air. She breathed deeply, savoring his scent.

His powerful, bronze chest mocked her. Annie swallowed and felt her mouth drop open. Oh geez. It was all she could do not to sway toward him.

She could not look him in the eye, certain of the mocking gleam she'd find there. She groaned inwardly. How would she ever get him back out? She'd be no match for him. His strength was blatantly obvious as his six-pack literally stared her in the face. A barrage of quick shallow breaths suddenly attacked her.

*Stop panting. Stay focused.*

She gazed in horror at his belt buckle. Should she stop? Cry uncle? *Daddy's Girl*, heralded through her brain like a clanging cymbal, calling her to action. No. She couldn't stop now. She licked her lips, then glanced at the doorway. Good, it was still ajar. Curiosity got the better of her and she stole a glance at his face. A slight smile hovered on his lips. She gulped and laid her fingers on his belt buckle.

"Not so fast, princess."

Her hands froze. Her eyes flew to his face.

"It's now your turn."

Smooth as silk, the words fell from his lips. She gaped at him. He placed his hand under her chin and closed her mouth. "That's better. Now you don't look so much like that red fish I caught last Sunday." He flashed a grin. "What? You didn't think this was going to be all one-sided, did you? My shirt is off and now yours has to come off."

"But, I'm wearing a dress. The whole thing will come down if I unzip it." She hated that she was noticeably breathless.

"Then I'll only unzip it part way. Like this."

He reached around her shoulders, encircling her upper body. She closed her eyes and with the finesse of James Bond, Levi unzipped her dress down to her waist. Thank

God, she had decided not to use the Band-Aids. Not that the low cut, lacy, black bra covered any more than a tiny patch of adhesive, but at least it was prettier and far less humiliating. She trembled and hated herself for being so naïve. *This is what you get for letting him think you're a slut.* He was so close she could feel the heat emanating from his body while his cologne sent shock waves down to her open-toed shoes.

'*The woodsy, earthy scent will drive her wild…for the lumberjack inside every man. Invisible Monster by Christopher Brosius.*' The TV ad spilled from her memory. She'd been the spokesperson for all their ads. The cologne was brand new. How in the world could *he* be wearing it? She kept her eyes closed and sucked in a breath when his fingers peeled the thin straps from her shoulders. She gasped when the fabric left her stomach and sides, settling on her hips.

"Princess. You awake?"

Her eyes flew open to stare at his bare chest. She stood there practically naked while his hands were still on her hips. Just one shove and her dress would fall to the floor. She raised her eyes to the hollow of this throat and swallowed. It took every ounce of self-control to keep from running her fingers along his collarbone, his wide shoulders. She raised her eyes to his chin, then his perfect mouth. Quickly. She had to work quickly, before she lost all her resolve.

With shaking fingers, she grasped his belt, then slipped the tongue from the belt loop. Her hands stilled. If pants could mock, his were certainly doing it. They dared her to continue. She sucked in a breath, held it, while she unzipped the front of his tux pants. Black tropical wool singed her knuckles before falling to the floor. She held her breath and watched him step out of them before kicking them aside.

He didn't say a word but his devouring eyes said plenty as he started to slide her dress over her hips.

"Wait. Stop."

"Stop? Honey, my engine's just now revving up. It'd be a shame to stop now, with the race about to start."

"The race?" She swallowed hard. "What race?"

"The one where you try to make a run for it."

She froze. Her rapid heartbeat the only thing moving. "Run?"

"Uh huh." He reached out and pulled her to his chest. She looked into his eyes and was utterly and completely lost. Run? Not a chance. His lips covered hers and all thoughts of running fled. Sweet surrender sang its age-old song as she melted against him. His kiss deepened, laying claim to hers just like Rhett claimed Scarlett's before he swept her off her feet and carried her to their bedroom. *Bedroom!*

Her eyes flew open. With his arms banded about her torso, skin against skin, she was powerless, at his mercy. She stared at him, wondering what to do next.

"Had enough?" His drawl sent her pulse into overtime.

"What?"

"Just how far are you willing to take this?" He cocked an arrogant brow, daring her to look away.

*Not that far.* She pushed him with all of her strength and he released her.

When he bent to pick up his clothes, reaction, swift and sweet took over. He stood on one foot and just as his long fingers looped around his tie, Annie yanked open the door, slapped both hands to his chest and shoved with all her might. Wide-eyed, he flailed backwards into the hallway. As he tried to right himself, she slammed the door in his face. With shaking hands, she slid the chain into place and collapsed against the door.

*I'm going straight to hell!*

* * *

"You little devil." Levi swore, righted himself and looked down the hall. He was never one to lose control but in that moment he came awfully close. Pounding on her door would only attract nosy heads popping from their rooms. He couldn't have that. He was the sheriff, for God's sake. He ran both hands through his hair and stood motionless.

He placed his knuckles to her door and gently knocked. "Annie. Open up. You know I can have you arrested for what you just did." He knew he couldn't but hoped she didn't. "Just throw out my clothes and we'll call it even." No response. Damn.

The elevator door opened. His gut tightened and he froze. A maid pushed a cart off the elevator. She turned, heading in the opposite direction. Relief soared. He hurried down the corridor, grabbed a bath towel from the cart and wrapped it around his waist.

"Excuse me, miss."

A young red-haired woman turned at his voice. "Sheriff? Is that you?"

*Oh, Lord.* "Yes, Millie, it's me." Good thing he'd taken a room here tonight. "Can you let me in my room? I got locked out."

"Sure thing, Sheriff." Millie followed Levi down the hall to his door. Thank God his room was on the same floor as Annie's.

She slipped her passkey in the lock. "Anything else?" she asked, as he stepped through the door.

"No, thanks." He turned back to her and caught the sparkle in Millie's eye. A look that clearly said she couldn't wait to tell this story.

He shut the door, pulled the towel from his hips, and tossed it over the shower bar in the bathroom. As he brushed his teeth, a pair of luminous eyes floated before his own. He swished, spit, then rubbed his hand over his mouth. He could still feel her lips. Could still taste the champagne and sweet icing from the wedding cake. He switched out the light, then fell back on the king sized bed. He punched up the pillow underneath his head and heaved out a sigh. Annie's warm, soft flesh, locked next to his had ignited nothing more than predatory instinct. He laced his hands behind his head. Purely biological. He thought about the day on the beach. How her green paisley bikini had drawn attention to every dip and curve of her beautiful body. He closed his eyes and groaned. But holding her against him with nothing but a lacy bra and half a dress between them was absolute, unadulterated heaven. But the rest of her? "Aggravating as hell." Staring at the ceiling, he could think of nothing else but a pair of golden eyes, pink lips, and smooth white skin that set his on fire.

# Chapter Seven

The following Monday morning, Levi parked in the space near the flagpole, then entered the non-descript redbrick, single storied building that was home to the Franklin County Sheriff's Department. He pushed through the double glass doors and entered the main waiting area.

"Morning, Sheriff." Jamie, one of the secretaries, raised her head from her computer and greeted him.

"Morning, Jamie." He nodded in her direction. She quickly lowered her head in what looked to him like an attempt to hide a smile.

As he entered the back offices, he was met with the usual hum of voices and the occasional slamming of a file drawer. But when he passed the command center, a hushed silence fell over the deputies hovering around their respective computers.

Why did he suddenly feel like the teacher who'd just caught his students cheating?

He slowed to a stop and briefly scanned the bodies hunched over the metal desks and Formica tables as if they were studying the most interesting case in the county. Something wasn't quite right but he continued across the floor toward the kitchen. His head ached and he needed coffee and an aspirin.

Sipping the steaming liquid, he left the break room, then entered his office to grab that day's file. After taking a few minutes to flip through it, he walked to the meeting room at the end of the hall. He was still perusing the papers when he stepped through the door. As he made his way down the right side of the room to the podium, he glanced over at the small group of male deputies seated at their desks. They were all shirtless. He blinked and stopped in his tracks. In unison, they stood to their feet, each wearing a bath towel wrapped around their waists.

*Dammit to Hell!*

Hoots and howls shot up from the group of men.

"We heard you got…*locked out,*" one of the guys yelled. Ear deafening guffaws and cackles rose to a high pitch throughout the small space.

"Hope you got your money back," someone shouted from the back.

"Knock it off, Dolan." More laugher. "All right, you've had your fun, now get your shirts on."

Levi walked down the center aisle and laid a manila folder in front of each man, trying like the devil to ignore the heat rising up his neck.

The guys continued to chuckle as they pulled off their towels. Every one of them had their green uniform pants on underneath and only needed to slip on their matching shirts. In a matter of seconds they were back in their seats ready for the morning session.

*　*　*

Levi pulled out of the station and headed down the highway. He needed fresh air after his embarrassing morning. As was his custom, he headed to Pearl's Diner. What he needed was Breakfast Special Number 5. Three eggs, bacon, sausage, with a side of pancakes. And coffee. Black and plenty of it.

He pulled into the gravel parking area and got out. When he entered the diner he took off his hat and sat at the counter next to the glass case that housed the largest pearl ever discovered in the area. It was displayed in the original oyster shell. Alice stopped on the way to her next customer and filled his mug.

"Back in a sec."

She flashed her pearly whites, the only thing white on her. Somewhere in her mid-fifties, Alice's dark leathery skin paid the price from years of over exposure to the sun, making her look ten years older.

Two minutes later, she was back with her pad and pencil. "What'll it be?" She stifled a grin.

He swore under his breath. "Not you, too."

"Dang, Sheriff, the whole town knows."

*Thank you, Millie Peterson!*

Alice leaned forward. "What was her name?"

"There was no her." Damn, he'd figured it would get around, maybe in a week or so, but this was less than twenty-four hours. He slapped his hat back onto his head.

"Can't hide under there. Everybody knows it's you. So, what'll you have? Number four, or five?"

"Five. Eggs over easy with an extra maple syrup." The diner served their pancakes with those small individual bottles of maple syrup and he found one was never enough.

"Number five, over easy," Alice yelled over her shoulder, then topped off Levi's coffee before going to the next customer.

* * *

Annie positioned Mark and Liddy's lounge chair directly facing the morning sun and sat down. After Liddy's wedding, she'd spent Sunday unpacking and settling in for what she'd thought would be two weeks of bliss. But after that unfortunate encounter with Sheriff Levi Hawke, bliss was long in coming. In fact it was nowhere to be found. She thought about the tux hanging in the guest closet with her things, and wondered if it was a rental. He'd need to return it soon or pay a late fee. Not that she really cared.

She stretched out, took a long deep breath, and exhaled. The Florida sun bathed her anxious flesh in a blanket of warmth, calming her a little. The sun began to seep every last ounce of stress from her body. What was it about the sun? So healing and yet so damaging to one's skin. She inhaled and tried to calm her worrisome thoughts. Thoughts that clamored through her brain like chattering squirrels, scurrying from limb to limb.

Chimes pealed through the house. The doorbell sent her heart racing like a frightened rabbit. Squirrels, rabbits. Next she'd be thinking of rats. A pair of ocean blue eyes and a stern uncompromising chin floated across her vision.

Bing a ding! There it was again. The chimes shot terror through her limbs. She'd been waiting for him to arrive.

Knew it was only a matter of time before he showed up. Probably with a warrant for her arrest.

She stood, slipped on her cover-up, and went to answer the door. Licking her dry lips, she placed her hand over her churning stomach and turned the handle. With the chain still in place, she cracked open the door. A mailman stood in front of her with a large package.

"Oh, just a second." She closed the door, quickly slipped off the chain, then opened back up.

"Here you go, miss. Have a good one."

She took the package and the rest of the mail from his outstretched hand. After shutting the door with her foot, she carried the mail into the kitchen. The package was from Nordstrom's. No doubt another wedding gift. She'd better get used to the doorbell as more gifts were sure to arrive while she was staying here. It would be crazy spending the week like some Nervous Nellie every time the doorbell rang.

She shuffled through the mail and tossed the junk, knowing Liddy would appreciate it. After stacking the rest of it next to the other boxes on the kitchen desk, she went back to the patio.

The sun was now overhead and after twenty minutes with it beating down on her, she decided to cool off in the pool. She padded over to the edge, then slipped into the water. She went completely under, then pushed off from the side, shooting through the water like a torpedo. After swimming several laps, she settled onto her back and relaxed into a float. When she neared the steps, she tilted back in the water, plastering her hair against her head and climbed out. As she walked back to her lounger, she caught her reflection in the glass doors off the patio. She twirled like she did on the runway.

She adored the energy and the excitement of a live show. Clothes flying off the racks. Strewn hangers, harried dressers aiding models, barking out orders. Trying to ignore the darting eyes of the male models changing nearby. She got a rush just thinking about.

Snatching up a towel, she quickly dried off and went inside to make lunch. After a quick perusal of the near empty fridge, she yanked open the middle drawer and pulled out the makings for a ham sandwich. She needed groceries. It was silly hiding out like a criminal. She'd have to face him sometime. In New York, the paparazzi lay in wait for her whenever she went out. Here it was Levi Hawke. It wasn't any different. Hiding was hiding. It didn't matter who from.

After she ate, she changed into shorts and a t-shirt. Donning her large, floppy hat, she slipped on her sunglasses and headed to the car.

Liddy's little yellow Fiat was parked in the garage. Annie climbed in. Literally. Since she was much taller than

Liddy, she had to adjust the seat as far back as it would go. It was tight but not as bad as she thought it would be when standing on the outside.

She crossed the small bridge that connected Mark and Liddy to the mainland, and was at Mel's Market and inside in no time. Mindlessly, she pushed the cart down each aisle, not sure what she even wanted. Always one to eat extremely healthy she was in the mood for something decadent. Pizza. She wanted pizza. With all the trimmings…pepperoni, sausage, extra cheese, red and yellow peppers, olives. Her mind reeled off all of the ingredients she wanted. After she found a pre-made one over in the deli section, she went to the outer aisle and bought salad fixings. At the back of the store she picked up a small package of fresh salmon. Pleased with her emotional compromise she added a few apples, then checked out.

Annie spotted the green and gold sheriff's car pulling into the parking lot just as she neared Liddy's vehicle. She skidded to a halt.

*Please, don't let it be him.* She blinked, picked up her pace, and got to the car just as Levi stepped out of his. She fumbled for the key and tried to balance the heavy bag of groceries on her hip at the same time. She looked over the top of the overstuffed bag to see where he was. Her stomach lurched. He was about to pass her. Maybe if she raised the bag higher. Covered her face. But as she did so the top-heavy bag proved too much. One moment, she was hidden from his sight and the next the bag toppled over, sending milk, apples, and pizza everywhere.

Annie dove for the milk, grabbing it just before it hit the pavement, then sunk to her haunches to pick up the rest. As she reached for the pizza, a pair of black shoes and green khaki pants entered her line of vision.

Levi bent down, grabbed a wayward apple before snatching up two more near his feet. "Here you go."

Thankful for the floppy hat, she kept her head lowered. "Thank you. I've got the rest of it." Her voice came out high and squeaky. Keeping her back to him, she scurried to grab the rest of the apples with one hand, while balancing the pizza with the other.

"I'll get that," he said as she reached for the car handle.

*Oh great! Just leave, already.*

Levi opened the door and held it so she could slip the bag inside.

"Thank you." She kept her head lowered and stood perfectly still, waiting for the inevitable.

He continued to hold the door open, as any normal, polite person would do. "Do you really think you can hide from me under that hat?"

She groaned inwardly. The jig was most definitely up. She raised her head *and* her chin.

"I figured you'd be long gone by now." He released the door and folded his arms across his chest.

"Yes. Well. I'm not." She looked him square in the eye and couldn't help notice the aggravated light in his. "Besides, why would I? It's beautiful here."

"Because most criminals flee the scene of the crime," he drawled.

"I didn't do anything wrong, except maybe steal your dignity. Last I heard that's not a crime." She clutched her purse strap, ready for battle. He couldn't make her leave. "You know what your problem is?"

"Please enlighten me."

"You're stuffy, rigid, inflexible, and arrogant. I bet you spend your days driving around, looking for someone to hound. You know, if you'd spend more of your time catching *real* criminals instead of tailing girls who are just trying to have some fun in the sun, I think you'd be a lot happier."

He shook his head. "You're all alike, you spoiled, high society women." His jaw tightened. "You think you can go anywhere and do anything without consequence."

"Are you stalking me?"

"Don't flatter yourself. This is a small community. But, I'll tell you what. You stay out of my way and I'll stay out of yours."

* * *

Levi was just as shocked to see her, as she apparently was him. With students and families visiting for fall break there were more female bodies in floppy hats than he could count. When he'd stopped to help her pick up her groceries, he had absolutely no idea it was *her,* until she avoided looking at him. As soon as he realized it, his blood pressure shot off the charts. He had been sorely tempted to escort her to the county line and tell her not to come back. Blood boiling, all he could think about was being pushed out in the hotel hallway in his underwear. The butt of this morning's joke still fresh on his mind, he decided right then and there, he would keep a close watch on her. She could go on thinking he was staying out of her way. Keep her off her red painted toes, as it were. He'd like nothing better than to catch her with her guard down. His heart raced, wreaking all manner of havoc on his inner region. It angered the hell out of him that she had that effect on him. He didn't like women like her. Not one little bit. A spoiled, daddy's girl was not for him. No siree.

He strode into Mel's Market and after grabbing an iced tea and a turkey sandwich he headed back to his car. As he pulled out of the parking lot he took a sip of the cold liquid. There were only a few places Annie could be staying. As he ticked them off in his mind, he spotted her at the Shell station just ahead in Liddy's Fiat. Of course, it made sense. But that didn't mean she was staying at Mark and Liddy's new place over on Bayside Drive. She could still be staying at the Sea Breeze Hotel.

He waited until she pulled out on the highway, then followed at a reasonable distance. She turned onto Sea Crest Drive, which led to the Bay Bridge. She was definitely going toward the Carmichael's home. From there, it would only be a short few blocks to Bayside and to Mark and Liddy's place. He made a U-turn and headed back to town.

* * *

Annie pulled into the driveway and parked in the back. It seemed she would be hounded here as well as in New York, only for completely different reasons. If he thought she was going to fall for that, 'you stay out of my way and I'll stay out of yours,' he could think again.

*Daddy's little girl.* If only she had been. As a kid, when she'd spend the night with her girlfriends, she'd watch them with their fathers. Longing for such a sweet, loving relationship with her own dad. She grew up wondering why it had been denied her. Wondering what she'd done.

She carried her groceries through the back door trying to dispel the raw ache in her heart. Most days she didn't think about her father or her childhood growing up in a home where anger and mistrust held court on a regular basis. After her mother died, it had gotten even worse. She realized her mom had tempered her father's outbursts and if not for her, Annie's life would have been far more miserable.

After putting the food away she poured a glass of sparkling water, added a dash of cranberry juice, then strolled out to the pool. It was near dinnertime but after her encounter with the *Sheriff of Nottingham*, she'd lost her appetite for everything, including pizza. He even ruined that. The more she thought about it the more steamed she became. She was Liddy's guest. How dare he make her feel like an intruder? Intimidate her with his 'me sheriff - you criminal' nonsense. Well, she had news for him. She would be going out to enjoy all that this little town had to offer.

Starting tonight.

# Chapter Eight

That evening, Annie dressed in a short, slinky dress. A hot pink, clingy thing that highlighted every one of her feminine curves. She'd bought it impulsively after modeling it for Marc Jacobs. She adored his clothes and couldn't wait for the spread in April's *Vogue* magazine. The theme was 'Sweet 'n Sultry for Spring'. She looked at her reflection in the mirror. It certainly was.

She took great care in applying her makeup. It had to be her most vampy and dangerous look. She smoothed dusty charcoal across her eyelids, then finished off with a deep glossy pink on her lips. She certainly didn't want to disappoint the good sheriff and hoped he'd be off duty. But finding him was another matter.

Annie climbed into the Fiat and headed to Coleman Drive. After twenty minutes of cruising up and down through town, she stopped at the Green Parrot Bar and Grill. She may as well have a nice meal.

When she entered she was met with candle lit tables and dark green leather chairs with brass rivets. Over to the right, there was a set of stairs that probably led to restaurant offices. Oddly, the whole place had a New York feel. Not at all what she'd expected for this area. You'd never know you were in a small fishing town in the Florida panhandle.

The place was crowded so she opted for a seat at the far end of the bar, near the stairs. After ordering a glass of Merlot, she sat back to relax. She was reaching for the menu when she noticed someone coming down the stairs.

Dressed in blue jeans and a white shirt, Levi Hawke clipped down the steps. She caught her breath. Gone was the green uniform and goofy patrol hat. He was casually dressed but there was nothing casual about what he was doing to her insides. From his short dark hair and broad shoulders to his muscular thighs. He looked amazing, a head turner for sure. Too bad he was such an arrogant jerk.

Lucky her, he was off duty, but her elation was short lived when she spotted his badge clipped to his waist. He was almost at the bottom step when he noticed her. He hesitated, clearly surprised to see her sitting at the bar. The look on his face was priceless.

Could she be any more fortunate? She smiled at him. A smile she knew blatantly boasted that she, Annie Dell, had caught him unaware and the feeling was pure heaven.

She slowly crossed one leg over the other before raising her glass to him in salute. She never took her eyes from his face and his eyes, Lord bless him, continued to bore into hers. It must really be hard for him not to have any reason to cuff her.

She turned to the man next to her and linked her arm in his. "Buy me a drink."

Surprise lit the man's ruddy features. He stared at her, dumbfounded.

"I'm trying to make someone jealous," she said.

"Oh, sure." He chuckled nervously. "I get it."

She could feel the electricity emanating from Levi as he approached.

"When's the baby due, Phil?" Levi asked.

Phil's ruddy complexion deepened even further and he hastily pushed her arm from his.

"Oops." Annie pressed her lips together and held back the smile that threatened to spread across her face. Poor guy. She had no idea. No telling what Robo Cop must now think of poor 'ole Phil.

"Evening, Sheriff." Phil quickly reached for his wallet, paid his bill, and left the bar.

"It's none of my business if you want to pick up married men, Miss Dell, but Apalacha Key is a small, close-knit community. I'd prefer it if you'd save your…nocturnal habits for some other town."

She felt badly for Phil, but this opportunity was too good to let pass. "But Sheriff, married men are so perfect. No strings you see." She raised her glass in salute and watched his eyes smolder as he turned to leave the restaurant.

Annie signaled the bartender for her tab. She pulled a twenty from her wallet and smiled. Levi's reaction to finding her with Phil was priceless. It was obvious she infuriated the good sheriff so what better way to entertain herself than to keep running into him, *accidentally*, of course. She slipped from the bar stool, secured her small purse over her shoulder and headed for the exit. It was time for some fun.

Levi pulled onto the highway just as she reached the Fiat. After she started the engine, she followed him out of the parking lot, but got caught at the next light. Squinting, she peered through the darkness trying not to lose Levi's taillights. Tapping her fingers on the wheel, she glanced between his taillights and the traffic light. It seemed ages before it finally turned green and when it did, she gunned it. When she reached Coleman Drive, she slowed to a cruise and perused the area. Other than the fact that Levi was extremely handsome, with the bluest eyes she'd ever seen, she had no idea what compelled her to chase after the man. It was foolish, even a bit reckless. It was clear he didn't like her, which made him all the more intriguing.

Minutes later, she spotted two Franklin County Sheriff cars parked next to each other at Sonic.

She slowed down to take a closer look, but sped past when she realized neither car was Levi's. She finally spotted him parked in the shadows at the next intersection. She shook her head. Sneaky devil. Just as she started to pass through, the 'No U-Turn' sign gave her an idea. That should get his attention.

She tugged the steering wheel way left, made the unlawful U-turn, then headed back toward Sonic. Talk about in your face. Just as she straightened the wheel, blue lights flashed behind her. She chuckled. *You're so predictable.*

Even though her action was a deliberate one, the flashing blue lights still set her heart pounding. After stopping, she gathered the necessary documents. The area was well lit and Annie could see perfectly the tall, very fit sheriff that stalked toward her. The streetlights reflected off the badge clipped at his narrow waist drawing attention to his physique. She wondered briefly why he wasn't in uniform. No matter, this was a much better look. She inhaled deeply, hating he had that effect on her.

Pressing her finger on the window button, she noticed abstractly how well her manicure was holding up and made a mental note to use that salon again.

*Okay, Annie. You're on.*

"Hello again, Sheriff." She gave him her most beguiling smile and handed him her license and registration. "We really should stop meeting like this." She propped her elbow on the door, her chin in her hand, and gazed up at him.

"Miss Dell." He dipped his head toward her. "You always seem to be in a hurry."

"Oh, you know how it is with us, *daddy's girls…*city girls. We have places to go, people to see."

She caught her breath at the intense gleam in his eyes. It was brief but challenging. *Bring it on, Sheriff. This won't be the first time I've taken on your type.* But something about the look in his eyes made her wonder if she wasn't about to stir up something she'd later regret. For one moment, a silent message passed between them.

"You made an illegal U-turn back there."

"Oh dear." She hated getting another ticket. She'd have to go to one of those dull evening classes to get it expunged. Small price to pay.

He tore off the ticket and handed it to her. "May I give you some friendly advice?" The question was moot because he continued without waiting for her reply. "If you're looking for a hot spot, I'm afraid we don't have any."

She shrugged. "Not that's it's any of your business, but I was going to Sonic."

He raised his brow and gave her a look that told her he didn't believe her.

"The coke floats are half price right now, so if you don't mind…"

"Of course. Watch out for the road signs. They're there for your safety."

Annie watched him stride off toward his car. Clamping her lips together, she shoved the ticket in her purse. She eased out and drove the last few hundred yards to the all night hamburger place. She parked in the first available slot. Levi followed, passing her car, before he slipped his vehicle alongside the other two squad cars. Three little sheriff cars in a row. What were the deputies talking about? She rolled down both front windows, welcoming the breeze, then leaned out to press the red button on the order screen.

"Welcome to Sonic. My name is Susan. May I help you?"

"Yes. I'd like a large coke float and a small fries, please."

"That'll be three twenty-two."

Three twenty-two. She wasn't surprised at how inexpensive it was. She'd grown up going to Sonic in Rockville, Iowa. As a girl she used to walk to one near her home, especially in the summer. The lowest prices in town and the food was really good. You could go out with your friends and not blow your entire allowance.

She climbed out of the Fiat to stretch her legs, then thought of another way to torment the good sheriff. Her dress was flashy and seductive so she might as well make good use of it. She strolled over to the other side of the outdoor seating area pretending to look for a seat. She turned, paused, and made her way back to the other side. Halfway back, she stopped at the center table where two men were eating. There was plenty of overhead lighting and she knew she'd be noticed.

"Excuse me. Do you know the time?" Annie fluttered her hand in the air. "My watch stopped." She hoped, from this distance, that it would look like she was flirting with the two men. Out of nowhere, a heavily bearded man approaching their table. His dark eyes narrowed when he spotted her, sending a shiver up her spine. She blinked rapidly, thanked the two men, and hurried back to her car.

While she waited for her order she noticed one of the men she'd talked to sliding a small package across the table to the bearded man that had approached them earlier. After he checked the contents of the brown envelope, he began arguing with the other two. Something caught her eye and when she glanced down, the bearded man had a gun pointed underneath the table at the other two.

Her pulse quickened and her legs became numb. Her breaths came quickly and she suddenly felt light headed. Time slowed as if she were watching the events unfold in slow motion. The gunman stood to his feet.

Oh, God. He was right in front of her. Feeling returned and she swiveled around in her seat. The sheriff cars were still parked a little behind her and to her right. If she could get their attention, then maybe—

"Don't even think about it." A gravelly voice interrupted her thoughts.

She whipped her head around to face the bearded man, now standing at her window. The gun was resting on her doorframe and pointing right at her. She froze.

"Open the door," he said.

"What?"

He leaned forward, jabbing the gun in her chest. Cold dead-like eyes stared at her. "Open it. Now."

The sudden onslaught of a dry mouth and weak limbs had her momentarily paralyzed. Her life flashed before her. Front page of the New York Times. 'Twenty-six year old ex-girlfriend of Alex Langdon, shot dead at Sonic while waiting for a coke float.'

Suddenly, there were two deputies on either side of the man with their guns pointed to his head. The man lifted his gun in the air, seemed to think for a second, before scrambling over the hood of the Fiat. There was a loud thud, then the man went flying. One second he was there and the next he was face down on the ground with deputies on top of him. Adrenalin pulsed through Annie's formerly stunned limbs. She sprang from the little car, then broke into a run, her strappy heels clicking madly against the blacktop.

* * *

"Annie!" Levi sprinted across the parking area, gaining on her in a matter of seconds. "Annie, stop!"

Drivers slammed on their brakes. Tires screeched. Levi grabbed her arm just as she entered the street and yanked her against his chest, almost falling over from the force of his own strength. He banded his arm around her small waist and held her tightly.

She screamed and clawed at his arm, but he kept a firm hold until he had her safely away from the highway.

"Annie. It's okay. You're all right. We got him."

She slumped in his arms and shook so violently that he had to tighten his hold while he walked her back to his car. Just as he got her seated, a young lady ran over with a coke. "Here, Sheriff. She might need this."

He took the drink and held the straw to Annie's lips. "Sip on this."

Her small hand shook as she reached up for the drink. He placed his hand over hers to steady it, and noticed the blood on her forearm. She swallowed, then leaned back in the seat. With shaking hands, she pushed her hair away from her face.

"You're bleeding." He pulled a first aid kit from the glove compartment. After swabbing the area with disinfectant, he taped a square piece of gauze over the small wound.

Annie lifted her elbow for a closer inspection. When she raised her luminous eyes to his, it was almost his undoing. He'd been terrified for her and when she bolted for the street, his adrenalin went into overtime. Part of him wanted to lecture her, another wanted to take her in his arms. He opted for the former and folded his arms across his chest.

"I'm sure you're used to being in the limelight. And, you seem hell bent on attracting attention. If you're looking for mine, you certainly have it. But, there are other, safer ways of getting it. Just something to think about."

He rubbed his hand around the back of his neck. "I need to leave you for a second. I'll be right back." He walked over to talk to his deputy, Lee Harris.

Lee was finishing up a note, then slipped the small pad into his shirt pocket.

"Talk to me," Levi said.

"The gunman and the other two have been cuffed and are now en route to county with Davidson and Sloan. The brown package contains heroine. Apparently, the gunman checked his package and found it lacking the appropriate funds. He pulled a gun on them and then tried to get away in Miss Dell's car. I'm going to interview the other witnesses." He nodded in their direction. "I should have more details later on."

"Okay. I'll see if Annie has anything else to add. See you tomorrow."

Annie was taking another sip of her coke as he stepped back to his squad car.

"What happened?" she asked.

"A drug deal gone awry." He gazed at her upturned face. "You were very fortunate tonight."

"I know." Her long manicured fingers gripped the medium sized coke.

"What did you say to the two who were seated?"

"I asked them for the time. And they told me. That was it. When I noticed the bearded man approaching their table I left. His eyes, they…" She shivered.

He tossed the pad and pencil on the front passenger seat. "Are you okay now?"

She nodded. "Yes. Thank you." Her large doe eyes looked up at him and held a question. "How did you know?"

"Earlier, when you turned and looked back at us, I saw the look of panic on your face. If not for that I would have simply assumed he was another one of your flirts." He was still angry and should have tempered his words, especially after what she'd just gone through, but the image of her throwing herself after Phil still angered him.

He watched the fearful, questioning light leave her face to be replaced by…could it actually be remorse? She lowered her head and seemed unusually interested in the drink straw. When she looked up, her shining eyes held a spark of challenge. She stood to her feet.

"Thanks for rescuing me, Sheriff. But the night is young. So, if you'll excuse me."

He was good at reading people and she was no exception. He knew for a fact she was bluffing and would be back at Liddy and Mark's as soon as she could get there. His eyes never left her face as she angled her chin even higher. He took note of the infinitesimal quiver in her bottom lip, knew her tears were not far off, and knew she would rather die than cry in front of him. He'd hurt her feelings. He was sorry for that, but someone needed to set her straight. She swiveled on her strappy heels and stalked to Liddy's car. Her body screamed vamp but her shimmering honey brown eyes and trembling lip told a different story. There was a warm, sensitive woman underneath that false front of hers. And God help him, he wanted to know more.

* * *

Annie backed out in one swift move then entered the traffic. Of course, she had no intention of staying out any longer. She couldn't wait to get back to Liddy's. She'd been such a fool. His comment that she'd wanted his attention galled her. That was the last thing she wanted. Well, she did want it, but not in the way he was thinking.

When she pulled in the driveway the house was in total darkness. She scanned the visor, then the dashboard for the garage door opener but couldn't find it. Why didn't she leave on some lights before she went out? Anxiety gripped her. Her chest tightened. She peered through the windshield into the black night. Darkness surrounded her. Indistinct shadows turned to creepy shapes. She knew they weren't real. Knew it was simply reaction to what happened earlier. She could still see the bearded man, the gun in her face. She quickly dug inside her purse for the house keys. She'd have to make a run for it. Then something hit her window and she froze.

# Chapter Nine

Levi gently tapped on the car window. Annie went rigid and screamed. He could tell the only thing keeping her seated was the seat belt.

"Annie, it's Levi. Open up."

Annie threw her hands over her heart and slumped back into the seat. Her hands shook as she fumbled to press the lock button in the door. As soon as it was unlocked Levi yanked it open, then unbuckled her seat belt.

She visibly trembled. A spurt of tears filled her eyes and he felt terrible. "I didn't mean to scare you. I was concerned about you and followed you home. I assumed you noticed I was behind you all the way here."

She shook her head and climbed out of the Fiat.

"Are you okay, now?"

She nodded and swiped at her check.

"That guy's locked up." When she didn't comment, he continued. "Come on, I'll walk you to the door. I'll even come inside and check it out for you if you'd like."

"Okay," she whispered meekly. Her unexpected compliance made him feel even worse.

When he'd opened the car door he'd fully expected her to lay into him for frightening her, but when she didn't a small part of him was suspicious. After all, it wasn't every day he got thrown out of a hotel room in his jockey shorts.

But her large expressive eyes and the slight trembling in her hands were evidence of her earlier scare. Either that or she was one heck of an actress.

He found himself softening toward her. Hard to believe this was the same woman making advances to a married man only hours earlier. But he wasn't a fool. It'd take more than one scare to change Annie Dell.

"Why didn't you pull in the garage?"

"I couldn't find the opener."

"We'll look for it inside," he said. "And while you're staying here you should leave a few lights on. The nights on the point are really dark without town lights nearby."

"I know. I realized that as soon as I drove up."

He pulled a pen light from his pocket and flicked it on while she unlocked the door. He went ahead of her and waited as she flipped the wall switch. Light flooded the kitchen.

"Come on. I'll walk through the house with you."

They covered the ground floor then went upstairs. After turning all the lights on and checking the closets they made their way back to the kitchen. He eyed her as she led him to the back door. He had no intention of leaving until she felt secure. He spotted a basket on the kitchen counter and rummaged through it. He held up the garage door opener.

"I'll be back in a sec."

Annie watched him flip on the garage light. Her large apprehensive eyes reminded him of his sister when she was little and afraid of the dark. He quickly programmed the opener, pulled the car in the garage, then came back inside.

"Done." He tossed the door opener back in the basket. "Will you be all right, now?"

"Yes. Thanks." She wrapped her arms around her torso. "I'll be fine."

"Okay." He nodded. "Lock up behind me."

"I will."

He stepped through the door and waited for her to lock up.

Annie stood inside the doorway, a slight frown on her pretty face. It was obvious she wanted to say something.

He stood there and waited.

"I'd like to apologize." The words rushed from her lips.

He blinked and stared at her, wondering if he'd heard correctly.

"You know" She spread her hands as if he didn't know what she was referring to. "For the other night."

Was she kidding? Did she actually think he needed reminding? That he could have possibly forgotten? Hell. It still chapped him to no end.

He crossed his arms and watched her struggle for the right words, not at all surprised apologizing was so difficult for her.

Up until now, he had just been doing his duty. His duty as sheriff and as a friend of Liddy's. At the reception Liddy had pulled him aside and asked him to keep an eye on Annie. Said that she'd been through a recent and painful ordeal. It was clear Liddy was worried about her friend. But thus far, all he'd seen was the behavior of a spoiled debutant. But at the memory of Liddy's clouded face and Annie's sudden change in behavior, he began to wonder what Annie's story was.

"...For locking you out. And for tonight, too." She was wringing her hands at this point. "Please don't be hard on your friend, Phil. I pretty much sabotaged him. He had nothing to do with—"

"It's all right, Annie." He decided it was time he came to her rescue. "Don't give it another thought." He reached in and flipped a light switch, turning on the floodlights. "Leave those on for the next few nights until you feel better."

She chewed on her bottom lip and nodded. Tonight's events obviously frightened her. Unfortunately, she was one of those people who had to learn the hard way.

After she shut the door, he gave her a second, then turned the knob, making sure she'd locked it. On the way back to his car he thought over the evening's drama. He was not much for baby-sitting but a promise was a promise. A part of him would be glad when Miss Dell's vacation was over.

* * *

Annie flicked out most of the lights in the house except for the one in the hall and at the top of the stairs. Safely inside the bedroom, she dragged the desk chair over to the door and shoved it underneath the handle. She knew it was silly, but it made her feel safer.

She sat on the edge of the bed and toed the heel of her shoes, flicking them to the floor, one at a time. As she padded to the bathroom, she thought about Levi. She'd met a lot of attractive men in her career but not one of them affected her like Levi Hawke. One minute he'd have her completely infuriated and the next he'd be standing there all male and magnificent and taking her breath away.

Like tonight. He had no idea how close she'd come to flinging herself into his arms. What would he have done if she had? Held her tightly? Merely tolerate her embrace? In that moment, with his broad shoulders and his badge clipped to his narrow waist, he absolutely glowed with protection. Like a shining knight from a fairy tale. Something she'd been looking for since she was a little girl. Unfortunately, she'd developed a knack for looking for him in all the wrong places.

Tears sprang to her eyes. She squeezed toothpaste onto her brush, then vigorously scrubbed her teeth. Shining knights were a fantasy and she knew from experience they did not exist.

Five minutes later she curled up in bed, then yanked the covers to her chin. Not until that moment did she freely give way to her tears. For the second time in her life, she'd come close to dying. She'd learned early on that a good cry worked wonders. The stress release benefits alone made it a worthwhile endeavor. She dabbed her eyes with the edge of the sheet. If she was going to keep butting heads with the sheriff, she'd better be prepared for a few more bouts, or at least keep a box of tissue handy.

# Chapter Ten

Annie woke up blurry-eyed and depressed. After she got dressed, she took the short walk to Owl's Nest, one of three neighborhood cafés on Pelican Point. A waitress, dressed in Pepto-Bismol pink, poured her a cup of coffee. Annie thanked her, took the laminated menu, and perused the breakfast options. A bulletin on the television mounted behind the counter caught her attention.

"Alex Langdon was arraigned today in New York for fraud and theft of 3.5 million in client funds." Annie froze and stared at the monitor. "Here, he's pictured with former girlfriend, and fashion celebrity, Anna Delany."

Annie stared at her latest glamour shot posted on the TV screen and slumped lower in the booth. Riveted, she watched the segment. The station flashed a series of photos of her and Alex at a recent fundraiser for Like No Other.

"Since the arrest of Langdon, Miss Delany seems to have disappeared from the scene. Friends say she is in seclusion and not working at this time. Now for the latest on tropical storm, Cindy…"

Annie tugged her ball cap over her forehead, slapped a five-dollar bill on the table, then hurried out.

That's it. She wasn't going out anymore while she was here. No more TV's or restaurants or anything. She had plenty of food and drink back at the house, a swimming pool, and a boat docked out back at Mark's private pier. What more could she want. She had six more days before she had to leave for her photo shoot in Miami. She'd stay put and try to relax in the few short days she had left, before she had to face the world again. Hopefully, when she came back to work with the girls, the fuss about Alex and her connection to him would be blown over.

True to her word, for the next several days, she closed herself off from the outside world. No TV, newspapers, and no Internet. She even shut off her phone, turning it on twice a day to check for messages from her agent about her upcoming Miami shoot.

Three days into her self-imposed exile, she awoke to a blanket of dark clouds. She padded out to the patio with coffee, plain yogurt, and fresh berries. After she ate, she slipped into her swimsuit for a morning workout. She'd found swimming laps was cathartic, especially lately. Being a swimmer most of her life, muscle memory stepped in and her body did all the rest. She swam lap after lap until she was in that in between state of energized and exhausted - that peak moment when endorphins flood your system.

She rolled over and faced the sky, allowing her heart rate to normalize before she got out of the pool. As she relaxed she took note of the clouds. They'd grown darker, more ominous. Signaling a storm for most, but a dire warning for her. Suddenly the sky opened and stinging rain spit on her upturned face. She blinked and righted herself. In two strokes she hoisted her body out of the water. Just as she stood, a gust of wind lifted her cover-up from the patio chair, landing it in a tangled heap on the concrete. She snatched it up, grabbed the coffee mug, then hurried inside. This could be a bad one.

She closed the French doors behind her and quickly toweled off. She'd planned to give herself a spa day while she was here and decided this was as good a time as any. Plus, it would help take her mind off the weather.

After hanging up the towel, she gathered her beauty supplies and set them out on the kitchen table.

Masques, firming gels, scrubs, and an assortment of nail polish covered the kitchen table. She opened the fridge and took out lemons, cucumbers, and the coffee grinds she'd saved each morning. Over the years, she'd learned to use natural ingredients on her body. While she organized her supplies, she thought about the girls signed up for her upcoming Like No Other sessions. She loved teaching teenage girls and the Miami shoot couldn't be over soon enough. As much as she loved modeling, she loved teaching the girls even more.

Looking forward to spending the next several hours in pampered heaven, she stripped off her bikini, secured her hair with a clip, then slathered an ample amount of body masque over her flesh. Orange and lavender permeated the kitchen. The heady combination relaxed and invigorated.

The avocado and lemon masque came next. Tilting the small table mirror upward, Annie spread the tangy green goop on her cheeks, chin, and forehead.

Her goal to be a model had taken root when she was thirteen. She'd gone to great lengths to protect her skin, pouring over fashion magazines, reading the latest tips and how-tos from the beautiful models that smiled at her from the glossy pages.

"Well, they worked, ladies. Thank you."

After rinsing off the body masque, Annie's flesh tingled with new life. She dressed in jeans and a sleeveless blue and yellow floral top, then gave herself a pedicure.

Ten minutes later, with the final stroke of the nail-brush, Pink Flamingo glistened from her toes. Annie sat back in satisfaction and turned on hairdryer to aid in the drying, while keeping her toes spread.

She glanced out the window. It was raining harder now and the dark clouds mirrored her growing anxiety. She hoped like crazy this would all blow over soon.

* * *

Perched on the edge of his desk, Levi, his small office staff, and three of his deputies, Dolan, Davidson and Sloan, watched the Governor of Florida go over evacuation routes and other pertinent information in regard to hurricane preparation.

The National Weather Service had issued a hurricane watch for their area several days ago. But last night that had changed to a warning when tropical storm Cindy had not only gathered speed, giving it hurricane status, but had changed course and was now headed their way. Building speed every hour, it was already stirring up a mess in the Gulf of Mexico. The sheriff's department, along with other emergency organizations and the police department, coordinated their efforts and reviewed rescue procedures.

None of this was new to Levi, especially having lived on the Florida coastline most of his life. He'd certainly experienced his share of storms. After fifteen years in law enforcement, emergency procedures and how to implement them were second nature. This wasn't his first rodeo and certainly wouldn't be his last.

"Okay, you know the drill." Serious, attentive eyes focused on him. "Rookies, listen up. Prepare your home and get your families evacuated. You're expected to work during the storm and the last thing you need is to be worrying about their safety. Then come back with your Disaster Supply Kit, your cell phone, chargers, an extra flashlight with batteries, and emergency contact numbers. When that's done, start canvassing the neighborhoods."

He handed each of them a printout. "Here's a list of the zones we're responsible for. Right now, we're still monitoring the storm. As you know, it could still change directions. Let's hope so." He turned to Jennifer his secretary. "Leave copies of the handbook for the others with a note for them to review it after they get back."

"Will do, boss." Jennifer took the copies from Levi. "Looks like we could be in for a long night. I'll make coffee."

"Jen."

She paused, then turned back to him.

"Go take care of your girls. I can make coffee." Something close to relief spread across her features. She was a widow with three little girls and way too young to have lost her husband to cancer.

"Are you sure? My mother's with the girls and she knows what to do."

"I'm sure." He smiled. The last thing he wanted was for Jen to be in danger.

Levi was no stranger to the pain and loss of a family member. The anguish on his parents' faces when they'd gotten the news of his sister's death still haunted him. He had no family here to worry about, so he may as well make sure Jen and her girls were safe.

He placed his hands on Jen's shoulders and gently pushed her out of his office. "Now, go."

Levi and his deputies left after the meeting to cruise their respective neighborhoods. Short gusts of wind did their dance of 'hit, then retreat' as he walked to his car. A sheet of newspaper tumbled across the pavement as if it was being chased. He glanced skyward. If the storm didn't change course by tomorrow morning, they'd certainly have their hands full with flying debris and flood-waters.

He got in his car, then headed to Market Street. The sound of hammers tattooed against wood like a million woodpeckers. Shopkeepers and merchants secured boards across windows and battened down anything that had the potential of becoming flying debris. The parking lot at

Mel's Market was already full as families loaded up on last minute food staples and extra batteries.

He passed the marina and thought about Mark's boat, making a mental note to check on it later. Mark's boat made him think about the Carmichael's house and…Annie. Surely, she had the sense to leave before the storm hit. But, being from New York, she might not understand the danger. He'd better check. He punched in Liddy and Mark's landline.

* * *

Wide-eyed, Annie watched one of the loungers tumble across the patio right into the French door. She yelped, shut off the hairdryer and jumped to her bare feet. While she stood transfixed the other chair slid across the patio like a paper cup before it finally flipped over in the pool. She slapped her hands over her ears. The chair tilted before it completely submerged like a sinking ship. She let out a breath, trying to stave off the rising tension in the back of her neck.

Her gaze traveled beyond the patio to the dock. White caps peaked and rolled across the canal water, while Mark's boat bobbed like a cork on a fishing line. Terror crept up her throat, suffocating her. She gripped the back of the kitchen chair. She was surrounded by water. A bridge separated her from the mainland. She tried to swallow but her throat felt like it was stuffed with cotton.

She ran to the sink, filled a glass with water, then nearly choked getting it down. Slamming the glass on the counter, she stared out the window.

Her mind whirled through time and space. She was ten years old. Locked in the shed. The smell of damp, musty earth tinged her nostrils. Torrential rains slashed like a thousand swords, thrashing the rustic boards until she thought they would rip apart. Water seeped underneath and began its slow march over her tennis shoes.

She bent over the sink, turned on the tap, and splashed cold water on her face. Scrunching her eyes shut, she coughed and choked over the waves of nausea that threatened to overcome her. To still the spasms, she sucked in one sharp breath after another. Beads of sweat broke out on her forehead. She clung to the sink trying to gain control, pushing the terrifying memory as far away as she could.

Finally, gaining awareness and some control over her body, she righted herself.

She blinked, took one last, shuddering breath, then yanked the shades over the glass doors. If she didn't have to see it, maybe it wouldn't be so terrifying. Months of therapy had taught her to handle most mild thunderstorms but the major ones still posed a huge problem.

She placed a trembling hand to her forehead and looked around the kitchen. Deciding to leave all the creams and concoctions to put away later, she hurried into the living room. She jumped onto the upholstered club chair, tucked her feet underneath her, and waited.

She'd heard typical Florida storms came and went quickly. She certainly hoped so. Although, this one seemed anything but typical. Her therapist had told her self-talk was important. Clasping her hands tightly in front of her, she repeated positive affirmations, focusing on her breathing as Doctor Eldon had taught her.

The affirmations began to take effect and she realized she needed to check the weather. He'd told her knowledge was power and being informed was half the battle. Weather updates were critical to good decision-making.

Just as she lifted the TV remote, the shrill ringing of the house phone made her jump. She clutched her floral blouse against her beating heart and stared at the receiver. On the fourth ring, she snatched up the sleek cordless phone and placed it to her ear.

* * *

Levi found himself counting each ring hoping like the devil she was already gone. It rang three times, a good sign she had already left. But, just as he was about to hang up, a voice, breathless and unnerved, answered at the other end.

"Hello."

Frustration filled him. "Annie?"

"Yes." Her breathiness turned to eagerness he couldn't miss a mile away.

"This is Levi. Are you all right?"

"Yes." She sounded winded and he wondered if she'd been working out. He waited for her to say more, then looked toward Heaven and rolled his eyes. She didn't sound all right.

"Listen, you need to leave town. A major storm is heading this way. If you leave right now, you have just enough time to get out."

Silence.

"Annie, are you still there? Can you her me?"

"I'm…I'm here."

She didn't sound 'here'. She sounded like she was somewhere else. Far away in fact. "Have you been watching the news? There's a hurricane in the gulf. It's heading our way. It's moving slowly and gathering strength. You need to leave. Do you understand?"

"Yes, yes. I do." There it was again. Breathless. Not the sultry voice she'd used on him earlier but fearful.

"Hey. There's no need to worry. The winds aren't that bad yet and most in the area are just now leaving. You'll be fine. Just don't dally."

"Okay. Thanks."

The receiver went dead. Her panting gasps cut short. She'd hung up. He stared at the phone in his hand. That was a completely different person than the one he had been dealing with lately.

She'd been nothing but trouble since she'd arrived. And, he had an uncomfortable feeling that trouble was exactly what he was in for.

# Chapter Eleven

Annie clicked on the TV and found the local weather. Her heart almost stopped at the sight of the massive, red and yellow graphic spiraling across the TV screen. It most definitely was heading their way. The reporter stated Cindy was heading northeast at one hundred and twenty miles per hour and strengthening. Hurricane Cindy. Really? You call that monster barreling toward them a Cindy?

She had no idea how long she sat there looking at the screen. But she wanted to find out everything she could about the storm before she had to get out in it. But the more she heard the less prepared she felt. If only someone were here with her. If only someone could drive her to safety. She wasn't sure she could do it by herself. She glanced at her watch. She'd been sitting here for more than thirty minutes.

"How was that possible?" She jumped from the chair and ran to the bedroom. She hurled the empty suitcase from the closet floor onto the bed. Arms flying, she stuffed designer clothes, shoes, purses and everything else she owned into the large case, heedless of the damage to the items.

The weight of the case nearly sent her sprawling when she yanked it off the bed, but she managed and pulled it down the hallway to the backdoor in record time.

She threw open the door and lugged the suitcase down the garage steps then stopped as if she'd hit a wall. Liddy's car suddenly looked very, very tiny.

Her heart sank. "Courage, Annie. You can do this."

She hauled the case to the trunk praying it would fit. After much pushing and shoving she was finally able to close the back hatch. She scurried in, strapped her seat belt in place and breathed a prayer.

Sheets of rain fell with blinding fury, pummeling the little Fiat as she backed out. How would she ever be able to drive in this? She set the wipers on high and pulled forward. Trembling, she gripped the steering wheel until her flesh turned white. She looked straight ahead but could hardly see a thing. Swish, swish. Back and forth. Her frantic heartbeat synced with the rhythm of the wipers. She crept along for nearly five minutes and had only gone a half a mile. After a few more minutes she reached the small bridge that connected Pelican Point to the mainland.

She clamped her teeth over her bottom lip. The sudden taste of iron sickened her. She winced and released her lip from between her teeth. She stepped on the brake and peered through the windshield, then slowly pulled ahead. Was that water on the bridge? It was so hard to tell. She leaned forward and swirled her hand over the windshield to clear away the frost, just to watch it fog back up seconds later. She huffed out a ragged sigh, turned the defrost on and waited.

She had no idea how long she sat there debating whether or not to try to cross. But drowning was not an option. At that moment, something caught her eye on the other side of the bridge. Car lights. She peered through the windshield and watched the lights go from low beam to high. Was the driver trying to signal her?

Just as she began to pull forward, a deafening crack followed by a thunderous explosion froze her to the spot. She slammed on the brakes and slapped her hands over her ears. Something ripped apart above her head. Terrified, she squeezed her eyes shut and cowered in the seat. A tree split into pieces, crashing on and around the car. She screamed.

Seconds ticked by. Random noises engulfed the little car. A slam. A crack. Splitting. Ripping. Pounding against metal. Her head jerked up. A tree limb buffeted the hood. Heart racing she stared through the windshield. A dark figure loomed in her line of vision. Someone was crossing the bridge.

* * *

The rain thrashed on and around the squad car as Levi pulled to a stop. As he peered through the windshield, his headlights revealed the fast moving water on the bridge. He'd hoped to be able to tend to Mark's boat sooner but canvassing the neighborhoods had taken longer than he'd expected. Nothing for it, he'd have to walk over.

He flipped the lights to high beam to access the water level, then spotted a dark mass in the distance. A tree had been uprooted and snapped in two, leaving a pile of leaves, limbs and tree bark in a tangled heap at the entrance to the other side of the bridge. A flicker of dim lights and glistening metal seeped through the mess and he could see a small car encased in the rubble. He hoped to God no one was trapped inside.

He grabbed the rope and harness from the seat next to him and got out. Lowering his head, he squinted against the pummeling rain and tethered himself to the railing. He braced himself and started across. Hand over hand

and one foot in front of the other, he slowly made his way to the other side.

As he neared the end of the bridge, he spotted the Fiat. *Annie.* His heart dropped to his stomach. Pelting rain stung his face while he quickly unclipped himself from the harness. As he pushed through the fallen tree, a sharp limb gouged his hip. He swore and grabbed his side, thankful for his thick rain gear. He sucked in a breath and maneuvered his body around the tree.

Levi wrenched open the car door, shoved Annie aside as if she was a feather and slid in the seat. How he managed to squeeze into the tiny car was beyond him. A canned sardine had more room than this.

The harsh glare of the overhead light spilled over Annie's ashen face. She blinked rapidly. After giving her a once over and satisfied she was physically all right, he brushed back the hood of his raincoat and laid into her.

"Are you crazy? Do you realize you could have been killed?"

Her violent shake of her head and tightly clasped hands should have been a warning signal. But he kept going.

"Why didn't you leave right after I called you?"

"I was afraid."

Annie's voice wobbled and her wide round eyes were filled with a combination of fear and relief. She was trembling and he wasn't sure if it was from fear of the storm or of him. But in that moment, he didn't care. All he could think about was that she was still on the island and all that was going to mean for the next thirty-six hours. Dammed right he was angry. He was now stuck with the unpleasant task of taking care of her. A silly, New York socialite. Yeah, he was pissed all right.

"Isn't there another way out?"

"No." he ground out, then shifted gears. "We need to go back."

"I don't want to go back. I want to leave." Her voice rose an octave.

"You've had days to leave. It's too late now."

He carefully backed the car away from the sprawling limbs. He hated driving these little things but right now he was never more thankful of anything in his life. "I could use your help. Check your side. I can't see a thing from here."

She peered out the window. "You're clear on my side."

He backed up and turned the car in the opposite direction, then looked over his shoulder at the tangled mass behind them. The tree had fallen on three sides of the car, if not for the size of this one, she'd have been trapped. A larger vehicle would have been crushed and Annie with it.

He glanced at Annie's profile. She stared ahead in sheer terror. Her right hand gripped her seat, her left splayed across the dash.

He pressed his fingers against his forehead. "We'll be at the house, soon." He needed her to stay calm. "It looks worse than it is." At least she hadn't gone into hysterics. But, by the look on her face, that could happen any second. It was all he could do not to slam his fist into the steering wheel.

With the Fiat now pointed in the opposite direction, he had them safely back in the garage minutes later. He climbed out of the Fiat, but stopped when he realized Annie hadn't moved. Wide-eyed, she stared in the side mirror and stayed put until the garage door closed behind them. As soon as the door hit the pavement, she sprung from her seat and rushed to open the trunk. He stepped around to help her but her small hand gripped the luggage handle beating him to it. It was obvious she didn't want his help so he let her have at it.

He watched her wrestle with her suitcase. Twisting and yanking on the oversized bag until beads of sweat formed on her smooth upper lip. It took every ounce of impulse control not to grab the damn thing right then and there. He folded his arms across his chest and waited, contemplating his next move. He was a patient man but this was getting on his nerves.

He counted to five. This was crazy. He reached for the suitcase. Just as his hand locked over hers, the bag broke free nearly sending her sprawling.

"I'll take that." He lifted the suitcase with one hand while steadying her with his other. "Let's get inside."

Annie flipped the switch and light filled the kitchen. A wave of citrus filled his senses. It smelled like fresh squeezed oranges and sweet lemonade.

"Where do you want this?"

"Please just set it down. I can roll it to the bedroom."

He nodded, gazing down at her. She stood hugging herself, staring at the floor.

"Look. I'm sorry I yelled at you. It was reaction." He waved his hand toward the garage. "I thought you were going to drive across the bridge in that bug of a car out there. When I realized you weren't hurt…" He let his words trail off. "Look, I'm not going to tell you that I'm not mad as hell right now. You and I both know that'd be a lie."

She raised her glistening eyes to his. "I know you think I'm an idiot. A fool. But, there's a reason I didn't watch the news. If I'd known about the hurricane, believe me, no power on earth could have kept me here." She lifted her hands as if that would help explain further. "I'm really sorry. I know you'd rather be anywhere but here."

Her voice broke. "And I know there are people counting on you and that I've made a muck of it."

Levi sighed and ran his hand across the back of his neck. She had certainly made a muck of things. He needed to be out there, but now he was stuck. With her.

She grasped the handle on her bag, but didn't move. "Thank you for helping me," she whispered.

"It's okay. We've been canvassing the neighborhoods all day and anyone who was leaving is probably gone by now. Even here at The Point, everyone's gone. Folks who live here know not to stay." He glanced around the kitchen. "Look, this was my last stop. Why don't you get settled and I'll make us some coffee. It's going to be a long night."

She started to pull her suitcase, then stopped. "Um, how did you know? I mean…that I was still here."

"I didn't. I assumed you were already on the road. I was coming to wench up Mark's boat. When I got to the bridge, the water was too high to drive through. After I realized there was a car stuck on the other side, I put on my waders and started across."

"You could have been killed." A fresh spurt of tears filled her eyes.

He gazed at her and something warm moved through his heart. Without makeup, she looked like a waif. Red nosed and God help him…adorable. His chest tightened. *Easy Levi. She's trouble, remember?* What was she saying?

"You could've been washed away in the canal." Her voice shook and her large brown eyes held a bucket full of concern.

"I tied myself to the rail, held on and moved across."

"Just to wench up someone's boat?"

Her incredulous expression brought a slight smile to his lips. "Hearing you say it does make it sound rather foolish, but I've been in situations like this before." He hoped his explanation would settle her a bit. Why he felt the need to ease her mind was beyond him. He told himself her large, soulful, brown eyes had absolutely nothing to do with it. She'd been nothing but a nuisance since the day they'd met.

Lightening lit up the evening sky. Annie sucked in a sharp breath, and like a frightened child, held her body rigid, waiting for the crack of thunder. All this fear and trembling seemed completely out of character for the woman he'd known thus far.

"Are we safe here?"

"For the time being. Yes." He opened one cabinet after another looking for the coffee. They were surrounded by water, but he didn't have the heart to tell her this was the last place they should be. But, if the storm slowed or turned west, they'd be fine.

"For the time being? What does that mean?"

He was trained to calm others in frightening situations and to control it in himself. He hoped like hell she wouldn't keep this up all night.

He pulled a can of Community Coffee from the cabinet. "It means we'll take things as they come. Let's see what we're up against. Turn on the TV. Right now, I have to wench up Mark's boat."

"You're going back out there?" Annie practically shrieked the question.

He glanced at the torrents of rain on the other side of the French doors. "I've been in worse. Look, I won't be long. Turn on the news and finish fixing the coffee." He hoped giving her something to do would help her not to worry so much. She was already a nervous wreck and the storm had barely started.

He held his breath and watched her. She stared up at him as if she were in some sort of trance, before she finally nodded.

"Good girl." Levi pulled his hood over his head and darted out the door. Hunched against the spitting wind and rain he made his way to the end of the pier.

* * *

After moving her suitcase to her bedroom, Annie hurried back to the living room to turn on the TV. The kitchen and main living area were connected so she was able to monitor the storm while she made coffee. She filled the pot with water, measured out the coffee, then pressed the power button. In seconds the aroma of fresh brewed coffee filled the kitchen. She turned toward the glass doors and waited. After a few minutes, she started to pace. Ten minutes turned to twenty and he still hadn't returned.

Three, six, nine. She counted her steps back and forth across the kitchen. Something had to have happened. Surely it didn't take this long to wench a boat. Glass shattered somewhere in the distance. She stopped in her tracks. The howling wind sent shivers down her spine. Pelting rain whipped and buffeted the house, closing in around her.

She wrung her hands. Where was he? Why was he taking so long? What if something happened to him?

Levi bolted through the glass doors as if Thor were after him. Annie shot like a bullet and flung her arms around him. Heedless of the rain pouring in behind them, she clung to his cold, wet waders, as if her life depended on it.

* * *

"Hey, hold on."
She'd almost knocked him breathless.

Annie took his words literally and clung even tighter. Surprise didn't even come close to the shock he experienced in that moment. The girl shook violently against him. He quickly closed the door, then wrapped his arms around her.

"It's all right."

"You were gone so long. I thought…" Fear tumbled from her lips. Her voice was high pitched.

"I'm sorry. I had to snap down the canvas. Try that in gale force winds. Halfway into it, the wench got stuck and I had to finish cranking it manually. But, I'm back now. And I'm not going out again."

He held her close and kept talking until he could feel her shakes subside. A moment later, he peeled her arms from his coat and put her from him. "You're all wet."

Large brown doe-like eyes gazed up at him before she glanced down at her clothes. "Is that coffee I smell?" She didn't answer, just kept staring up at him. "Why don't you go change and I'll have the coffee poured when you get back. Do you take cream, or sugar?"

"Yes." Breathless, her doe eyes continued to gaze up at him.

"Yes, cream, yes, sugar or yes, both?" he asked.

"Both. I take both." Her eyes fluttered downward and she stepped away from him. "I'll go change." Annie ran from the kitchen.

He watched her go, not quite certain what to make of what just happened.

He stripped off his wet jacket and waders and threw them over a peg in the laundry room. Trying to shake off the imprint of Annie's soft curves and trembling body, he opened the fridge and set out the cream. *That woman is trouble and don't you forget it. Get your mind back to the business of survival.* He pulled himself up short, still able to feel the trembling curves plastered against him. He heaved a sigh. Heaven help him. He'd survive the storm but would he survive her?

# Chapter Twelve

Two mugs were already sitting on the counter, so he spooned in the sugar, then added cream to both. Just as he poured the hot coffee into the second mug, Annie appeared at the entrance to the kitchen.

Dressed in black sweat pants and a pale pink t-shirt, her comfortable outfit did little to hide her shapely curves. She stood poised, barefoot and motionless in the doorway, her bright worry-filled eyes stared at him as if she were waiting for permission to enter. She'd pulled her long, dark hair back into a ponytail, making her look much younger than the siren from yesterday.

"Let's go sit down." He picked up both mugs of coffee, then followed her to the living room.

Something whistled past the front door. He paused, a mug in each hand as Annie leapt onto the sofa, curling up in a ball at one end. Her lips began to move but he heard no sound. He wondered if it was some mantra to calm herself. Then it finally dawned. She wasn't afraid of storms - she was terrified of them. And here they sat, stranded on an island with a Cat 3 hurricane coming their way. Good Lord above. He was not looking forward to tonight.

As he waited for her to come back to the present, he wondered what in the world had happened to her to make her this frightened.

Half an hour later, they were staring at the TV, watching the stream of traffic heading north on the interstate. Levi was thankful the local stations were still viewable.

"For some reason it doesn't look that bad." Annie sipped her coffee. "I guess I overreacted. But, too late to think about that now." She shook her head.

"What?" he asked.

She lifted a slender shoulder. "I was just wondering if I should have crossed the bridge when I had the chance." She waved her hand at the TV screen. "If I hadn't hesitated, I could be there right now."

"That's way inland. Those cars have been on the road for at least two hours."

"All the same, I wish I'd acted sooner." She bowed her head, her manicured fingers encircled the mug.

"Hindsight is always twenty-twenty. You did the right thing. The water on the bridge was quite forceful and believe me that Fiat would have floated away in seconds." *And you with it.* But he kept that tidbit to himself. No need to alarm her more than she already was.

She glanced at the news program on TV. "There's Dave Cannon. I can't believe he chooses to be in this mess."

He smiled. "I wouldn't worry about him. These weather men take plenty of precautions in something like this." He sipped his coffee and continued to look at her.

"Oh yeah, cautious. That's Dave all right."

He raised a questioning brow at her. "You know him?"

She ran her finger over the rim of the mug and stammered. "I…dated him once."

"Only once," he said. "And you already have that nice negative opinion of him."

Her eyes lifted to his. She pursed her lips and set down her mug.

"Okay, it was more than once." She laced her fingers together and slid her hands between her knees. "But believe me, it was long enough."

Suddenly, all kinds of tormenting images of Annie and Dave floated across his mind. "Sounds interesting. Anything you'd like to confess to the local sheriff?"

"There's nothing to tell, he was just one more jerk in a long line of jerks."

He wondered if he should be a gentleman and change the subject but she did that for him.

"I have your tux, by the way."

"Speaking of jerks?" he said.

The corners of her mouth lifted and she flushed a delicate pink. My God. She was growing more and more adorable by the hour.

"It's hanging up in the back bedroom closet. You might want to take it when you leave."

She didn't look at him. Not once, during her little speech.

"Did you iron it?" he asked.

Her head shot up. "No."

The look on her face clearly said she thought he was crazy. He held back a grin at her irate expression. She flushed even deeper when she realized he'd said that merely to get a reaction from her.

"You sure do rise easily."

She scowled, then gnawed her bottom lip. "Ouch!" Her hand flew to her mouth.

He'd noticed earlier her lip was bruised. "How'd that happened?"

"I bit my lip, earlier." She grimaced.

He reached into his pants pocket and pulled out a small tube and handed it to her. "Here. Put some of this on."

She took it and read the label. "Antibiotic gel." She unscrewed the cap. "This is convenient."

"Just use a small amount."

"Do you always carry stuff like this in your pocket?"

"You'd be surprised how many little skinned knees I come across in my line of work." He glanced at her bruised lip. "Don't let that get in your mouth."

Annie squeezed a tiny glob on the tip of her index finger, dabbed it on her lower lip, then handed the tube back.

"So. What happened afterwards?"

Levi paused with the mug near his mouth and glanced at her. "After what?"

"You know." Her pretty brows arched and her full lips tilted upward. "After you were out in the hallway?" Her smile echoed in her dazzling brown eyes, sending heat waves across his gut. Even the purple and red whelp on her lip didn't take away from her beauty.

He set his cup down, folded his arms across his chest and leveled a look at her that he kept in reserve for his rookie deputies. "Without going into details, I'll admit I'm still smarting from that experience."

"Oh." She lowered her eyes but not before he saw the merriment in them. She bit her lower lip, again. "Ouch." She threw her fingers over her mouth. "I have got to stop doing that."

"Don't think your time isn't coming."

Her eyes widened and locked with his. She swallowed, then blinked. All traces of humor suddenly left her beautifully, scrubbed face.

* * *

She couldn't blame him for wanting some payback. But after overhearing his comment at the rehearsal dinner, she'd made it a point to prove he was right about what he'd thought of her. She pursed her lips careful not to hurt herself this time. Really stupid, now that she thought about it. Most women would want to disprove a comment like that. But she wanted him to think he was right in his assessment of her. She wasn't sure why unless it was so she could turn the tables on him at a later date. But it seemed the tables were now turned on her. Here she was, stranded with him. Alone. At his mercy. She was a fool to think she could hurt the Sheriff of Nottingham by her childish actions.

She glanced over at Levi's lean, well-put together body. He was tall, and certainly dwarfed her five foot eight inch frame. Her heart thudded just thinking about how she'd clung to him only moments ago. How she thought she could ever turn tables on *that* was beyond her. She must have been suffering from some malady.

An ear splitting crack of thunder exploded over their heads. She gasped and jumped. Tension oozed from her body. "It sounds like the sky is splitting apart."

He leaned forward in his chair and placed his forearms on his knees. "It's going to get a lot worse as the night progresses. Even into the morning. You're going to hear noises that you've never heard before. Foreign, frightening sounds. As the storm moves in, you're going to think the roof is ripping from the rafters, which means it probably is."

She felt sick. He might as well have just told her that she only had hours left to live.

# Chapter Thirteen

"Would you like more coffee?"

She shook her head.

"Do you have anything in that giant suitcase of yours to help you relax?"

"We're going to die, aren't we?" She jumped up like she'd been sitting on a spring. "There's wine in the fridge. I'll get it."

She bolted for the kitchen. Seconds later she returned with the wine and an opener.

"When I suggested you take something to help you to relax, I was thinking more like a prescription."

"Drugs?"

He nodded, eyeing her carefully.

"I don't do drugs…at least not in a while." She held out the wine to him.

He stared at her wondering what the heck she meant by that statement. "No thanks," he said. "I'm still on duty."

"Well, I'm not. Would you please, open it?"

Stubborn didn't come close to describing her stance. Her question sounded more like a command. She was not going down without a fight. If drowning your fears was fighting, that is. Against his better judgment, he took the bottle from her and screwed in the opener.

The cork squeaked along the glass and with a final tug Levi slipped it free. A quick glance at the familiar label told him it must have been left over from Mark and Liddy's wedding. He looked around for the glass and was surprised when Annie took the bottle from his hand to take a generous swig.

"Hold on," he said. "I'll go get you a glass."

When he returned, Annie was back on the couch in her little corner of the world with the bottle to her lips. He eyed the glass in his hand, set it down, then watched in amazement as she downed about a fourth of the wine.

Just as she raised the bottle back to her lips, he leaned forward and lifted it out of her small hands.

"Slow down."

She yanked it back, startling him. "I'm in a hurry, if it's all the same to you."

He pressed his lips firmly together and lifted the bottle from her fingers. "Sorry, but I'm not going to stand here and watch you get plastered." He re-corked it. "At least, let that take effect before you down any more."

Her eyes flashed daggers and her pink lips turned down in a frown. "Give it back."

He shook his head and just stood there looking down at her.

She leapt to her feet. "I said, give it back."

She snatched at the bottle, but he raised it high out of her reach, all the while watching her get madder and madder.

She stood rigid, her hands clenched by her sides. "I'm not going to ask again." She held out her hand, which mirrored the direct challenge in her eye.

Anger and fear was an unhealthy combination. One that usually led to injury or worse. And she had it in spades. He needed to diffuse this. Hell, he was worried, too. A category 3 hurricane was heading their way. He was the sheriff and unavailable to his deputies and to his community. She wasn't going to budge. Well neither was he.

Her chest heaved and she continued to give him the evil eye. Fine. He'd make the first move. Hoping she, too would back down. He lowered the wine bottle to his side. Just as it neared his waist, she lunged for it. Her hand brushed the Glock 21 strapped to his hip. Years of training took over. Levi grabbed her wrist, pushed her down on the sofa and before she could blink, cuffed her to the leg of the end table.

Annie gasped. Her wide, frantic-filled eyes lifted to his face. Her head snapped back down and she jerked her arm over and over but the only reward for her efforts was the tightening of the cuffs around her wrist. Desperation turned her golden eyes to dark amber. With her other hand she pushed and pried the cuff trying desperately to pull her wrist free.

"We have at least twenty-four more hours together and this is not how I'm going to spend them. Do you understand?"

Annie's face crumpled and she burst into tears.

Levi sat down on the chair opposite her, ran his hand down his face and watched her. Broken, heart-wrenching sobs poured from her lips. Which he chalked up to reaction and too much wine.

Suddenly, she yanked on the table so hard the lamp teetered on its edge. Levi jumped up and caught it just as it tipped over, then placed it on the floor out of harm's way. To say that he was surprised at her explosive behavior was putting it mildly. Hell. It wasn't like he'd hurt her. And it wasn't like she couldn't easily get free, either. If she'd just stop and think for a second, she'd realize all she had to do was lift up the table leg and she'd be out.

Sobbing, she yanked and jerked against the cuffs. She obviously needed to cry. Needed to get all the fear out. So, he sat there and waited. But after twenty more nerve-wracking seconds and loads of self-guilt, he'd had enough.

"Hey. Hey, look at me." He knew he had to win if they had any chance of making it. Before this night was over he would need her and she would need him. It was imperative she was sound and cooperative. If this storm worsened, it would take both their wits to stay alive.

She hiccupped, shuddered, then wiped her eyes with her free hand. Raising red-rimmed eyes to his face, she yanked once more on the handcuffs. "Take these off," she demanded.

"Not until you're completely calm." He thought she was going to start bawling again, but instead she swallowed and wiped at her eyes. "I…I need a Kleenex."

He handed her two tissues from a floral box on the opposite end table. She blew her nose, then sat looking at him in anticipation of her release.

He stood over her never taking his eyes from her face. When he was satisfied she was in control of her emotions, he slid the key from his pocket. Placed it in the lock and freed her.

"Sorry about that. But you gave me no choice."

A shudder coursed through her spent body. "I was going for the bottle." She massaged her wrist and glared up at him.

Her dramatic, accusatory tone was just another notch in his sheriff's belt. Another affirmation of his reputation as the tough and unbending sheriff. It was how he kept citizens alive and safe. And how he managed his own personal demons.

"Your hand hit my gun," he said. "I wasn't taking any chances."

"Why do you hate me?"

Surprised, he stared at her. Was he that obvious? It was true. He didn't like her. She put on airs and thought she could manipulate the male sex with a single bat of her inky lashes and her pink, pouty lips. He absolutely did not like her, but hate? No. He didn't hate her.

"I don't hate you."

She rubbed her hand over her chafed wrist and stood up.

He glanced at the red marks. Remorse tugged against his insides. He sighed and slipped his hand into his pocket.

"Here." He pulled out the tube of antibiotic salve. "Give me your hand." When she wouldn't comply, he took hold of her arm and pulled her back down on the sofa next to him.

* * *

She had no choice but to stretch her arm out over his lap. She sniffed. "Feeling guilty?"

Levi glanced at her and unscrewed the lid. He dabbed antibiotic cream on her wrist. His strong hands were unexpectedly gentle as he twisted and turned her wrist to cover the red marks.

She gazed up at his face, surprised to see it clouded with concern. *Yep, he was feeling guilty.* Frown lines creased his forehead, a furrow deepened between his remarkable eyes. She caught her breath. They were amazing. The deepest blue and absolutely gorgeous. She wondered how they must look when he smiled. For some reason he chose to live with a constant furrow in his brow. She glanced down, focusing on her wrist and his tender hands. Tender. Now that's a word she hadn't thought she'd ever use when describing him.

"There." He stopped his dabbing to screw the cap back in place. "It really wasn't that tight, you know. If you hadn't pitched such a fit this wouldn't have happened." He stood. "Your struggling only made it worse."

She had pitched a fit, which was not at all like her. Maybe, he just brought out the worst in her. She rubbed her wrist and looked right at him. "If that's your way of apologizing, it's no wonder you have a burr up your butt."

Silence.

Her heart stopped. *Did she just say that out loud?*

"What did you say?"

She clamped her teeth together and gazed up at him. A tall, forbidding. Stranger. He may as well be anyway. What did she really know about him? She gulped. "I said, it's no wonder you have a burr up your butt."

He burst out laughing. He actually threw back his head and laughed. She blinked. This was not the reaction she expected. The physical change in his features was astonishing. His usually stoic face lit up with genuine laughter and his eyes held a contagious twinkle, transforming him into utter gorgeousness.

Muscles tense, jaw clenched, she'd been ready for battle. Not to have the wind knocked out of her. She heaved an internal sigh and her legs turned to mush.

"I deserved that." He stated with such a matter of fact tone that she wondered if she'd entered a parallel universe.

He looked down at her and the most amazing thing happened. He smiled. An actual, honest to goodness smile. Not a smirk or a sneer, but one that lit up his eyes.

A breath gasping,

Heart stopping,

Faint at your feet,

Smile.

"Are you hungry?"

Was it her or did his voice take on a smoothness she hadn't heard before? Kind. That was it. He sounded kind. He leaned forward at the waist and placed his hand under her chin, closing her mouth with the touch of a finger.

"Don't look so shocked. I am human, even though there are those who may not think so. Including you and your precious Liddy."

Something crashed in the distance. She stared at him. He folded his muscular arms across that broad chest of his and just stared back at her, as if waiting.

"What?" she asked.

Another slow, heart-stopping smile spread across his face.

"Nothing. Come on." He glanced at the TV, then headed for the kitchen. "Let's find something to eat."

She trailed after him, not at all comfortable with that knowing smile planted on his face or his sudden kindness toward her. He was up to something. Nobody changes that quickly. What was it he'd said earlier? Her time would come. She'd have to watch him, and closely. Sheriff or not, she wasn't about to trust him willy-nilly.

When she entered the kitchen he was already setting out some bread and cheese slices.

"Can you cook?"

"If you mean, can I make cheese sandwiches, then yes, I can cook."

He slanted her a look that she was, unfortunately, becoming very familiar with. "You asked me a question earlier. And, while I don't 'hate' you, I certainly can't say that I like you. Especially, when you resort to sarcasm every time you open your mouth."

"Oh, come on. Surely not *every* time?"

"See what I mean?" He held a bread slice and pointed at her. "Just like that."

"But, what about you? 'Can you cook?'" She mimicked using a deep masculine voice. "Look, just because I'm a model—"

"An honest forthright question, right to the point." He set the mustard and mayonnaise on the counter. "I've never been one to beat around the bush."

"I can certainly believe that." Annie opened an upper cabinet, rummaged through the canned goods, and found some tomato soup. "Do you like soup with your grilled cheese?"

"Grilled? That sounds good. And yes, soup sounds great."

"We might as well have hot food while we still have electricity."

"Good thinking."

She gave him a doubtful stare, openly displaying her suspicion.

"I see a big fat question on that face of yours." He grinned. "Care to ask it?"

"It's just odd. You making small talk." She shook her head. "This whole experience is crazy. I'm stranded in my best friend's house with Buford Pusser himself, who gave me, not one, but two tickets, and within mere minutes of the other. And a hurricane is…" Her hand stilled over the bread and she glanced at the French doors. "…right outside my window."

The wind was getting stronger and something was knocking against the back of the house. Suddenly, all of the outside noises mushroomed into gargantuan significance. She gazed up at Levi, looking for comfort. He was eyeing her and she could tell, he too was holding his breath.

"I was hoping it would last longer than that," he said.

She licked her lips. "You were distracting me all this time?"

He nodded, his blue eyes never leaving her face.

So, there was a sweet side to Robo Cop, after all. "And when you cuffed me?"

"That was for real, I'm afraid." A deep twinkle appeared in his eyes.

She pursed her lips. "You're something else, let me tell you." She shook her head. "Just like the day you pulled me over."

"What about you? Batting your beautiful eyes at me. Smiling coyly. Thinking it would what? Keep me from doing my job?"

*He thinks my eyes are beautiful?*

He took the bread from her and was spreading mayonnaise on it seemingly unaware of what he'd just said.

She drew in a steadying breath, blinked rapidly, and swallowed. "Heaven forbid, someone should keep you from doing your job." She exhaled slowly, but her heart seamed hell-bent on that persistent fluttering. "I can't imagine anyone ever doing that." She poured the canned soup into the pot, willing her heart to slow down.

"Exactly."

"Especially, some saucy little maiden," she said.

"Especially, that." He looked over at her with a teasing smile on his lips.

"Or, some…spoiled daddy's girl." There it was out. The thing that had bothered her the most. Words both unfair and untrue that stung and hurt more than she could say. Words that took her to a place of both fear and dread.

The teasing light went out of his eyes. "You heard that?" He set down the knife, turned and looked fully at her. "So, that's what this is all about."

She glanced away to attend the simmering pot of soup. "Yes." She continued to stir the smooth red liquid. "There's a reason daddy's girl is particularly hurtful, if you must know."

"I'm sorry. First impressions are sometimes hard to ignore. Especially, in my line of work."

She shrugged. "It's okay. I'm guilty of doing the same thing. I didn't think too highly of you either."

"How about now?"

She removed the spoon and tapped it on the side of the pot. She was so very thankful he was here and that she was not alone. "The verdict is still out." Was all she said, even though she felt a small tug on her heart. So. He'd been trying to distract her. She licked her sore lip. There were other ways of distracting someone. She took note of his tall, very fit frame and wished like crazy he would take her back in his arms. Imagine that. In the arms of Robo Cop. That would certainly get her mind off of things.

## Chapter Fourteen

After the sandwiches were made, Annie ladled up the soup. Just as she was carrying the bowls to the table, a deafening bang blared outside the patio doors. She froze in her tracks.

"Here. Let me take that." Levi gently took the bowls from her hands and set them on a tray. "You'll hear things like that a lot tonight. Let's eat in the living room. Away from all of this glass."

Annie didn't need to be told twice. She grabbed the drinks and hurried from the kitchen. Levi set the tray on the coffee table and pulled up a side chair. Annie sat on the couch, her outward calm shattered. Back were the wide eyes and the ghostly complexion. She sat rigid, on high alert. Like radar, tracking the oncoming storm.

"Buford Pusser *and* Robo Cop." He hoped to distract her. "As a fan of both, I consider myself in good company, but somehow I don't think that was your point." He gazed at her but she wasn't paying him any attention. Well, no one could say he hadn't tried.

"This looks good." He dipped his spoon into his soup. "Don't let yours get cold."

"Huh?"

"Your soup and grilled cheese. Eat up before they get cold."

She nodded, picked up her spoon, then dipped it in the savory liquid. He watched her covertly from where he sat across from her. In the kitchen, he had enjoyed their casual banter. For the first time, he felt she'd revealed a glimpse of who she really was. This woman, he could get interested in. Not the flirty, contemptuous female she'd been up to this point, but the honest, open-hearted woman she was at this moment.

She toyed with her spoon taking only a few bites before she reached for her sandwich. He needed to distract her. "Look at that weather guy. Cannon is it?"

"Yea."

*Come on, kid, relax.*

"He's out there. We're in here. Who's safer?"

She fluttered him a smile. It was tremulous and sweet. There was no doubt her wide-eyed fearful restraint had awakened his protective instinct. She was undeniably the most beautiful woman he'd ever seen, even now, with her candid display of anxiety clouding her features.

Suddenly, he wished he knew her well enough to take her in his arms. Wished he'd not been the one that had pulled her over. Wished their first meeting had been at Mark and Liddy's wedding. Things most definitely would've turned out differently. She'd be in his arms right now instead of cowering in the corner of the sofa, picking at her food, fearing for her life.

He glanced at her plate. She had eaten half her meal when the TV screen suddenly turned into white noise.

"What happened?" Panic squeaked from her lips.

"We've lost reception. It happens all the time in a storm. Come on, you know that. Take a deep breath, Annie. You're all right."

She looked at him. "I know. It's just…I'm afraid of storms," she blurted out.

*No kidding.*

He watched her take a deep breath. Like the one he'd seen her take earlier. The subtle movement of her lips told him she was repeating her mantra. He wondered what it was. It must have worked because she visibly calmed and raised her eyes to his.

"I'm sorry. You must think me a fool, being so frightened."

This was more than a typical fear of storms. "We're all afraid of something."

"I can't imagine you being afraid. You're tough and unflappable. You exude self-control. It seeps from your pours like sweat. A stark contrast to my pathetic weakness."

"Wow."

"You know you are. Robo Cop." She twinkled at him, in spite of her fear.

"Ouch. Now, I've gone from tough and unflappable to unfeeling and robotic. Is that how you think of me?"

She glanced at the bowl cupped in her hand.

"I did."

She raised her eyes to his. The fear had taken a back seat to something else. Honest regard. Her trusting glance both humbled and saddened him. She was in for a terrible night and he didn't have to heart to tell her just how bad it was going to get. To be this frightened when the storm had barely even hit land. He sighed inwardly. He didn't want to think what it would be like for her when the full impact was upon them. But maybe, before the night was over, he'd get to hold her.

* * *

After they finished dinner, Annie made coffee and cleaned the kitchen while Levi went to the garage to see if he could find anything useful in case the lights went out. Filling a thermos with most of the coffee, she split the rest between two mugs.

Levi pushed through the back door carrying a large box. She quickly set the mugs on the counter, then held the door for him.

"I found this." He nodded to the box in his hands. "It's full of camping supplies." He set the box on the kitchen table. Inside were two lanterns, a Coleman stove, butane canisters, as well as various smaller cooking utensils, and some freeze-dried packages of food.

"Mmm, this looks pretty good. Chicken tetrazzini." He lifted another. "Beef stew with Portobello mushroom sauce." He glanced at her with those all-seeing eyes of his.

She dropped her eyes from his intense gaze and reached inside the box. She was so embarrassed by what other's coined 'her irrational fear' of storms. She knew they were anything but irrational but that didn't make her nearly *losing it* in his presence any easier. She'd never done that with anyone in her life, not even with Liddy. She was proud of the fact that she hid her demons from the world. Ignored them unless she was completely alone, and even then, she rarely gave into them.

Her father had been the irrational and emotional one in the family and she never knew when he'd fly into one of his rages. Most of her childhood had been spent in fear of when those rages would happen. She'd hold her breath wondering if this event or that event would set him off. It wasn't until she was older that she realized his *episodes* were linked to his abuse of alcohol.

She realized she was playing with the contents of the box and lifted her eyes back to Levi's. He was staring at her, assessing her like a bug under a glass. She cleared her throat. "This looks especially delectable." She forced a smile and held up the package of campsite brownie mix as if she were on TV, then read the label like she was doing a commercial.

She set the packet back in the box. It was obvious from his expression she hadn't fooled him with her forced smile and silly antic.

"You know. Keeping busy helps. Maybe later we could unpack some of Mark and Liddy's boxes for them?"

"Good idea. I've unpacked most of them in the living room and kitchen. It was the least I could do for them."

Levi pulled two small flashlights from the box and flicked each one on, then off. "Here." He handed her one. "Keep that with you at all times."

"Okay." She pushed a lose strand of hair behind one ear and handed him his coffee. "Watch it. It's still hot." She sipped the caramel colored liquid and went back to her spot on the sofa. Levi followed with a small radio he'd pulled from the box.

"Let's see if the batteries are any good." He held the radio in his lap and pressed the power button. Static blared from the small speaker. The irritating noise crackled on and off as he scrolled to find a local station.

"There. Stop," she said.

A male voice spoke through static from the small speaker. '…And heavy rains have spread well ahead of Hurricane Cindy. The threat of flooding along Cindy's path is very high - sustaining winds of up to one hundred twenty-five miles per hour. Strong gusts will continue to cause tree damage and power outages. Expect large waves and a destructive storm surge along coastal areas. Cindy is expected to make landfall after midnight.'

Annie gazed at Levi. His expression was grave and his eyes held a note of concern as they focused on the radio.

"That doesn't sound good," she said.

"It's not." He turned the sound down, low enough for them to still hear it, then set the radio on the table.

* * *

"The eye is coming right for us." Speaking of eyes, Levi watched hers fill with dread. "The good news is it appears to have lost some strength and there's always the possibility it could turn again. Any slight shift in direction and the bulk of it could miss us completely. You know how they can be."

"Not really."

She stared up at him, concern etched in every corner and crevice of her beautiful face and hanging onto his every word as if he had all the answers.

"Annie, listen to me." He grasped her hands and gave them a comforting squeeze. "This house is brand new. Built on twelve pylons that are twenty feet into the ground. It's built to withstand hurricanes. Sure it's going to get beat up, and it may take on some water, but it was built to stand in just such a situation as this."

Her serious big brown eyes bore into his and it was all he could do not to pull her into his arms. How the heck did he get here? God alone knew how badly he wanted her at this moment. In mere hours, he'd gone from wanting to arm-wrestle her to wanting to kiss her fears away. Right now, he'd like nothing better than to give her fearful brain something else to focus on besides that blasted Cindy. But, he knew he couldn't. To give in to an emotionally charged moment was not cool. Besides, he was still on duty.

He stood. He needed to put distance between them. "Stay here. I'm going to check the attic."

He hadn't gone two steps when she appeared at his side. She didn't say a word, just saddled up close behind him. He hesitated but kept going. She was scared and he couldn't very well tell her to go back. Even though she lost her bravado during storms, he wouldn't put it past her to resurrect it, if only to shoot down his order to stay put. She didn't take orders very well and damn if he didn't admire her for it. But, best for her not to know that.

The pull-down attic door was at the end of the upstairs hallway. He flipped on the light and climbed up the steps. Seconds later, he felt her weight on the stairs behind him. So much for putting distance between them. Now, he'd be closeted with her in the tight space of the attic. He welcomed it but for completely differently reasons than she did.

When he got inside the attic he turned to give her a hand. "Steady. You'd think as many years as they've made these things, they'd be more stable than this."

There were two dormers at the back with windows that opened to the sloped roof. Except for three boxes, marked 'Christmas', the space was empty. Levi walked over to one of the dormers and looked out the window. He couldn't see much but could tell they could get to the roof if need be.

"It's worse up here," she said.

He turned toward her.

"The noise. It's too much," she said. "I'm going back down."

She practically fell over one of the boxes in her haste to get out.

"I'm coming, too." He climbed down before her, then held the stairs as she made her descent, stepping back as she neared the floor. Just as he folded the steps and door into the ceiling, the lights went out.

Levi quickly switched on his flashlight. The beam hit Annie in the face and she squinted against the white glare. "Well, we knew this was coming." He spoke lightly and kept talking as they made their way back to the living room.

"I'm okay, it's not the dark that scares me. But it does seem to amplify the situation."

"It does, doesn't it?"

They entered the living room to the low hum of the voice on the radio. Annie sat back down while Levi lit the candles and turned on the lanterns. Annie had spaced them in the room earlier and now the soft light took on what normally would be a romantic setting.

The wind howled and screeched like the soundtrack of a horror film, bringing random slamming noises in its wake. Annie wrapped her arms around her torso and dropped her head to her chest. A low moan escaped her lips as tears coursed down her checks. "I'm sorry."

Levi was next to her in seconds. He gathered her in his arms and drew her to his side. God, she was sweetness itself. How could he have thought otherwise?

He held her tightly and pressed her head to his shoulder. Silence. He'd hoped she would open up to him, instead, she clung to him like a lost, frightened child. Inconsolable sobs wracked her entire body. He lifted her onto his lap and held her tightly. She was tearing him up. He could understand being frightened, but this was different.

As an officer, he'd experienced weeping couples, children, and grandparents. Especially those who'd lost a loved one. As difficult as those times were, he'd been trained to keep a professional distance.

But this?

Her.

He couldn't help himself. He was falling, because she was taking him with her to a dark and painful place.

# Chapter Fifteen

*What happened to you, Annie?* Unable to take his eyes off her, he watched her. She wept with such vigor and abandon, that he didn't know which was louder, her or the storm. He kept his arms securely around her, until, spent, she shuddered against him.

Her right cheek rested just below his shoulder. With her eyes closed and her full lips slightly parted she was beautiful. A real sleeping beauty. Waiting to be kissed awake. Did that make him Prince Charming? He grimaced. He was no Prince Charming. She'd called him an unfeeling brute. She'd referred to him as Buford Pusser and Robo Cop. He lifted his hand to brush a wayward curl off her cheek. *Feeling* all sorts of emotions at that moment. If she could read his thoughts, then she'd know how much he could feel. She would know that right now, his heart ached to protect her, to kiss her. Even now, knowing it was inevitable, his heart raced in anticipation of the very moment when his lips would finally claim hers. He placed his fingers along her tear-streaked cheek and when he brushed them away, she opened her eyes. He continued to hold her and frankly couldn't get enough of her. His eyes roamed over every inch of her lovely face. She blinked uncertainly and pushed out of his hold.

He released her and she slipped from his lap to the seat next to him. She clasped her hands together and stared at the floor, clearly at a loss for words.

"Are you okay?" he asked.

"Yeah." She gave a quick nod, as if she were frantic to assure him of that fact.

Dear Lord, he wanted to take her back in his arms. Kiss her until she lost all fear of the storm. Assure her she was safe with him. That he was an experienced law officer. Knew what to do in an emergency. Fully capable to handle this hurricane and all it would certainly bring. He stood.

"I'm going to see if Mark has anything I can wear. I think it's safe to say I'm off duty now."

She gazed at him, all wide-eyed and lost, breathtaking in the candlelight. He turned on his heel to escape.

He flicked on the flashlight as he made his way to the back of the house, wondering how many more excuses he was going to have to come up with to put some distance between them. He hadn't been this attracted to anyone since he'd entered puberty. When her brown eyes lifted to his with that 'please don't leave me' look, it was all he could do not to crush her to him.

Brushing his hand through his hair, he entered the master closet and almost tripped over the unpacked boxes stacked at his feet. Lifting the flashlight, he scanned Mark's cloths. Grabbing a pair of jeans and a navy blue polo shirt off the rack, he tossed the flashlight on the bed, then changed.

When he walked back in the living room, he skidded to a stop. "Annie?"

"In the kitchen," she yelled.

She popped her head around the door, the thermos in one hand and two mugs in the other. "Here, take this, while I grab the cookies."

He did as he was told, a bit surprised at the change in her. The unwelcome thought that she'd been faking it crossed his 'officer of the law' brain. But he immediately rejected it. Her sobs were real. She was definitely terrified of storms. Besides, he'd always heard a good cry worked wonders. Maybe that's what caused the change in her.

He balanced the thermos and mugs with the flashlight and followed her to the sofa, then sat down across from her.

"These look fantastic."

She looked inordinately pleased.

"I baked them yesterday."

"So you *can* cook."

"Yes. It's amazing. I can actually read and follow recipes."

She bit into the large chocolate chip cookie, slapping her hand against her mouth to catch a piece that had broken lose.

"Moist little devils," she said.

Was it him or had she suddenly become a chatterbox? Then it hit him. She was nervous. He glanced around the room. "It seems brighter in here."

With a mouth full of cookie, Annie reminded him of a chipmunk. She had to wash it down with coffee before she could speak.

"Yeah, I put some more candles out while you were changing." She shot to her feet. "Would you like another cookie?" Her question did little to cover the uptight figure that stood before him.

"If you give a mouse a cookie…"

Her soft lips quirked appealingly. The mention of the well-known children's book bringing a small smile to her lips. Her entire body relaxed and he was rewarded with the merry twinkle that suddenly lit her eyes.

"I suppose that means you'd like a glass of milk." Her smile broadened and a rosy pink filled her cheeks, the candlelight making her all the more beautiful.

She was suddenly the cutest thing he'd ever seen. Lord, what had gotten into him?

"I used to love that book," she said.

"My sister loved it, too."

"You have a sister?"

"I used to." *Hell. He never talked about his sister. Not with anyone.* "She passed away."

"Oh, I'm so sorry."

"Thank you, and yes, I'd love another one." He wanted to change the subject and stop any questions. "And, I'll take that milk if you have it? It's rare that I get home-made cookies *and* milk."

"Really, I would've thought home baked goods were a daily occurrence in a small town like this."

"One would think," he said.

She was back with another cookie and set it on his plate. "And here's your milk." She curled up on the couch and stared at him.

"You're not having another one?"

"No." She placed her hand against her stomach. "I've probably added a pants size this past week alone." Her laugh lit up her eyes and he responded with a smile of his own. She amazed him. What happened to the terrified little girl from earlier?

From siren, to scared little girl, to flushed-face virgin. Will the real Annie Dell please stand up?

Levi washed down the last bit of cookie with the milk she had served him just as the wind began to pick up. He leaned forward and turned up the volume on the radio.

'In other news, Alex Langdon pleaded not guilty in court today to three counts of fraud and one count of theft. Ex-girlfriend, Anna Delany is still missing in action. The socialite model was last seen entering Langdon's brownstone in Manhattan, more than two weeks ago. Her agent told ABC news that she is vacationing at a private home, taking a much needed rest.'

He glanced over at Annie. She was ghostly white and sitting very still.

Oh my God. He knew there was something familiar about her. That day on the beach when he'd thought he'd seen her pose before. He had. A similar photo of her had been plastered on the news during the past month. How could he have missed it?

Annie Dell was Anna Delany.

High fashion model. Wealthy in her own right, girlfriend of that scumbag, fraudulent real estate tycoon, Alex Langdon. He'd seen her in those provocative poses with expensive, extravagant dresses, plastered all over the national news. How could this scrubbed-faced, frightened girl, who looked nothing like the woman in the fashion magazines, be Anna Delany?

He clenched his jaw. He'd been duped. Sucked in by her big brown eyes and full pink lips. Cuddling and caring for this…siren. As for thieving, well the verdict was still out as far as he was concerned.

"If you were trying to hide your past, I would have picked a different name. Annie Dell is much too similar to Anna Delany."

# Chapter Sixteen

Annie stiffened. The cool change in his demeanor was not lost on her. Nor the raw edge to his voice. He spat out her name like spoiled food. *Not him, too. Please, not him.* Not after how he'd made her feel.

Levi stood and began pacing the floor. He wouldn't look at her.

"I just wanted the wedding weekend to be free of whispers and finger pointing. I only wanted to be able to look into someone's eyes and not see condemnation. It was never my intention to deceive you or this community. I never thought I'd be here long enough for it to matter, either way."

She watched him wear a hole in the carpet, then he stopped and locked eyes with hers.

"So you had nothing to do with Langdon's schemes?"

"That's right. I've been questioned by both the FBI and the police and found innocent."

"Then you won't mind if I do my own investigation."

She sucked in a ragged breath. "Of course not. *Sheriff.*"

"And your fear of storms? Is that even real?"

She stared up at him. Square jawed and immovable. He was back to his old hard self. She'd thought he was different. His own man. "You're just like everyone else. Judgmental, non-trusting, and narrow-minded. Believing I'm guilty by association."

She waited for him to say something, but he stood silent. Any peace she'd found that night was suddenly shattered. His accusatory tone and the raging storm swirled and broke through her protective shell, smashing it to smithereens.

She didn't know which was worse, to be frightened or depressed? But she'd get no comfort from him. Snatching up her flashlight, she ran down the hall to her bedroom. Once inside, she leaned against the door. Running. She was always running. The wind whistled outside her window and something slammed against the house. She sucked in a breath and cringed. Gale force winds shook the house and rattled the windows. Desperation won the moment. She grabbed a pillow off the bed and clutched it to her chest.

With eyes squeezed shut, she hugged the pillow even tighter, cringing at the unholy sounds outside. She sobbed and dove under the desk.

* * *

Levi stalked to the kitchen and poured himself a glass of merlot. He gripped the counter and downed half the glass, but even that didn't quell his rising anger. He took another sip and stared at the wall. He'd been played and that he couldn't forgive. He'd been a fool to fall for her.

The wind had picked up and buffeted the house like crazy, ripping and tearing until Levi thought the house would explode. His neck and shoulders ached from the tension. He poured another glass and wondered if Annie really was terrified of storms, or was that a sham, too. Another ploy to get under his skin.

But as soon as he thought it, he knew it wasn't true. She was terrified all right, and probably going through hell right now. He swore and set down his glass. He didn't know what was real, but no matter what he thought she'd done, he was a public servant and never knowingly let another human being suffer if he could help it.

With determined steps he strode down the hall to her bedroom. He didn't knock, but walked right in. The bed was empty. So was the chair in the corner. The wind roared like an oncoming train. Fear gripped him and slammed his gut. Heart pounding, he stepped further into the room and finally spotted her underneath the desk next to the bed.

*Sweet Jesus.* She was curled up on the floor, cowering near the wall, her face hidden in the pillow clutched against her chest. In two seconds, he was down on his haunches beside her.

"Annie." He spoke softly. She was frightened enough already and he didn't want to startle her. He reached under the desk and touched her arm. Her head jerked up and tears streamed down her checks. His heart dipped and turned a summersault. "I know it sounds really bad, but you're safe. I promise. Have you tried quoting your mantra?"

Her head jerked a sharp nod. "Yes." Her face crumbled. "But it's not working."

"Come here." He reached for her but she shrank away from him. "Annie, I'm sorry." And he was. Even though he was still angry about being deceived, it was important they stick together. He kept his hand out toward her and watched her face for the smallest sign of surrender. When she released the pillow and swayed toward him, that was all the signal he needed. He pulled her out from under the table and into his arms.

"Hold onto me," he said. He leaned against the wall and held her close. She clung to him in holy terror. Her hands fisted at his chest. She was as stiff as a body in the morgue. "It's okay. We're safe here." He kept his voice calm and soothing. He rubbed her back and could tell she was responding to his systematic strokes. After several minutes, she was very still. *Too* relaxed. "I know you're not asleep so stop pretending."

Her eyes fluttered open. "I'm okay." She pushed out of his arms and scooted to the side of the bed. She drew her knees to her chest and leaned back. "Really. You can go. I know you don't want to be here." Her voice was low and raspy.

"Give it up, princess. We're in for a long night. Best if you stay right here." He patted his chest. He could tell she wanted to. But she wouldn't budge. Then the wind howled like an injured wolf shaking the house to its foundations. She yelped and flew back in his arms.

The sound penetrated deeper, like helicopter blades surrounding the house. Whosh, whosh. It grew to *freight train* proportion that whistled and raged on the other side of the wall. It reverberated the entire house *and* inside his head. He gripped Annie tightly and held on. The wind wailed like a thousand sirens. She threw her hands over her ears.

"Levi!"

"Right here, honey." He had to yell over the noise. Tension wracked his own body and truth be known, he was as thankful to be holding her as she was him. At that moment he wasn't quite certain who was holding on to whom.

A lull. Finally. The train sounds lessened, but he had no idea for how long. Annie clung to him, warm and trembling, doing things to his insides no woman had ever done before. He'd hold her all night if he had to. He wasn't a monster. He definitely had more questions and would deal with them later, after the storm was over.

# Chapter Seventeen

Annie's eyes fluttered open. It was pitch dark. She sat up with a jerk and glanced around the room. The storm. It was still raining but it didn't seem to be as bad. Maybe the worst had passed. At least she hoped it had. She was in bed but didn't remember how she got there. Levi must have carried her. She threw off the covers, grabbed the flashlight and went to the bathroom. Her hand went immediately to the light switch. Still no power. She leveled the flashlight at her watch. Five forty-five.

She thought about the moment Levi discovered her identity and groaned. She'd had no idea her celebrity status would cause such a reaction from him. The hurricane had her in such a state that it never once crossed her mind to mention it. And why should she? She hadn't done anything wrong. It wasn't like her deception was diabolical.

Rubbing her hand across her forehead, she made her way down the hall to the living room. The lanterns were still on and the candles were burning low. Levi was in the process of setting out more.

"Is it over?" she asked.

He turned when she spoke. "I think we're in the eye. If that's the case, we're half way through it. There's nothing but static on the radio so I don't know for sure."

"Oh."

"After we eat, I'm going to try to get to my car radio." He spoke abruptly and walked back into the kitchen.

Annie followed behind him for some water.

When she entered the kitchen he was firing up the portable stove. He glanced over his shoulder and gave her a quick perusal before turning his attention to the carton of eggs at his elbow.

As she was standing at the sink filling up a glass, he tore off a wad of paper towel and stuck it under the tap. He wrung it out and handed it to her.

"You might want to wash your face. You have raccoon eyes." He spoke blithely and went back to his cooking.

She glanced in the small mirror that was still in the kitchen from her spa day and groaned. Streaks of black mascara had smeared underneath her lower lashes. Placing the damp towel underneath her eye, she gently rubbed back and forth, but in the low light couldn't tell if she was getting it.

"Here. Let me."

Before she could say no, Levi plucked the dishtowel from her fingers, placed his free hand under her chin and tilted her face toward him. He wiped the area below one eye. "What's in this stuff, glue?" He ran the damp towel across a bar of soap, then continued to scrub underneath her eye.

"Ouch. Stop." She pulled away. "You'll give me wrinkles."

He gripped her chin between his fingers. "Hold still. I almost have it."

She scrunched up her face against his administrations.

"There. Done." He tossed the towel in the trash.

Tongue-tied, she stared at his retreating figure. He was a hard man to figure out. Tender one moment and tough the next.

"Breakfast is almost ready," he threw over his shoulder.

She sat down at the counter. Her shoulders and neck ached from holding herself in a tight ball most of the night. Except for the short time he held her in his arms. That was heavenly. For one long blissful moment she had transferred her fear onto his broad, capable chest. Just knowing he'd had the strength and fearlessness to handle it had comforted her. Is that what a knight does? Protect his maiden from the storms of life. No, not from, but through. There would always be storms.

She stared at his square shoulders and broad back. The man standing there scrambling eggs had no idea that for one moment he had been her shining knight. But that moment was long gone. Now his dislike and mistrust screamed from his broad-shouldered, uncompromising stance. Better for him not to know that she not only liked it when he held her, but loved it beyond anything imaginable. Hard not to with the wind constantly howling like a banshee from hell, and her along with it. She grimaced at the memory. She knew, as an officer of the law, he'd acted out of duty and nothing else. Even though he'd held her with a stiff formality, it hadn't mattered. He was warm and strong and alive.

She busied herself getting the forks out. It was better than sitting there thinking.

"Is that coffee I smell?" she asked, in an attempt to make conversation.

"It is."

She filled a mug, savoring the aroma. After a generous sip, she closed her eyes in ecstasy. "Mmm, nothing like that first sip to wash away the dregs of sleep."

"Yeah, takes the morning growls away," he shot stiffly over his shoulder, as he scraped the eggs onto the plates.

He shut off the stove, then turned hard blue eyes in her direction. Robo Cop had returned.

It hurt her terribly that he thought so badly of her. Even though it was mostly her own fault. In the hotel room, he'd asked her if she really wanted his attention that badly.

*Yes.*

She stared into her coffee cup while a large masculine hand placed scrambled eggs, bacon and toast in front of her. He was eyeing her with that cop look, or should she say, sheriff look. Like he was waiting for her to do something wrong. Just one step out of line. Then bam! Book 'em Danno.

"This smells wonderful." Hickory smoked fatback seasoned to perfection filled her nose. "Do you realize how many years it's been since I've eaten bacon? I saw it the other day and couldn't resist buying it." She hoped some light conversation would lessen the tension between them.

"You mean that wealthy thieving scoundrel you date doesn't buy you bacon?"

She inhaled sharply and her heart dropped to her stomach. "Oh, he buys me bacon, all right." She snapped off a piece with her fingers.

Levi's jaw clenched and his eyes darkened.

"I wondered when the real Annie would show up." He tossed the dregs of his coffee into the sink.

"Would you at least like to hear my side of things?" she asked.

"The rain is letting up. I'm going to my car to see if I can get through to my office. Clean up while I'm gone."

He pulled on his rain gear and slammed out the back door.

"I guess that means, no." She slumped in her chair. The sooner this was over, the better. Putting up a front was dizzying. She couldn't wait to be alone again, so she could be her plain old boring self.

* * *

He could not get emotionally involved with her. At least, no more than he already was. When she entered the kitchen, it had taken every ounce of cop-control not to sit her down right then and there and ask her a hundred questions. He needed answers. Her involvement with Alex Langdon, for starters. Personally and professionally. Instead, he'd deliberately kept his back to her. Knowing, if he looked into those big brown eyes of hers, he'd be lost.

Levi parked the Fiat near the felled tree and got out. The floodwater had receded considerably but still moved fairly quickly. He untied the rope and harness from the rail, gathered it to his chest, then took his time crossing over. When he was safely across, he hopped in the squad car.

He grabbed the radio. "Lee. Come in."

"Levi, thank God, you're okay."

"I'm fine. I'm at Pelican Point, at Mark and Liddy's new place, over on Sea Breeze Drive. I got stranded."

"How'd that happen?"

It's a long story. I'll fill you in later. Is everyone okay at your end?"

"We're all fine," Lee said. "So far we've had only one casualty. An elderly man on Compton had a heart attack. Not sure if it was related to the storm, though."

"What's the storm report?"

"Good news. Cindy shifted so we caught the eastern tip of the eye. And she's slowed considerably. So the tail end is shorter and is now at tropical storm strength."

"Which means we should be able to drive in it sooner than later." Levi said.

"We?"

"Yeah. Liddy's maid of honor is at the house."

"Anything I can do to help?"

"No. We'll be fine for a few more hours."

"Okay. Be safe, bro."

"Will do." Levi hung up the hand unit and waded back across the bridge. For the next twenty minutes he cruised through the neighborhood to see if anyone needed assistance, but the island was deserted.

Back at the house, he parked in the garage, then walked around Mark and Liddy's property, cleaning up what he could. Mark's boat was nicked and scarred pretty badly, but nothing that couldn't be repaired.

When he got back inside, Annie was still sitting where he'd left her. She stood when he entered.

"I reached my office. The rotation of the storm has slowed considerably, so I'll be leaving in about thirty minutes. As soon as the storm clears out, there'll be clean-up crews all over the area."

"How long before we have power?" she asked.

"It depends on the damage. Hopefully, not too long."

She nodded.

"Look, if you'd rather not stay here, you're welcome to come back into town with me. I can take you back to the hotel."

"No. I'll stay here."

She licked her lips, slid her hands into her back pockets and gazed up at him with those big brown eyes of hers.

"It is over, right?"

He'd be lying if he said those Bambi eyes didn't affect him. Still laced with worry and lack of sleep, they tugged on his heart like a lost child tugs on a police officer's hand. For a second, he stood there battling an array of emotional impulses. Better to put distance between them until he could think more clearly.

"The worst part, yes. What's going on outside will become less and less, then it'll be over." He crossed the kitchen, holding the portable radio. "Have you checked the weather?"

She shook her head and splayed her fingers across the counter.

He turned it on and static filled the room. "Why don't you see if you can find anything, while I change."

She nodded but didn't say anything.

"Look if you're worried about being left alone. Don't be. The storm is well past."

"I know. I'm okay."

She was far from okay. Her eyes pleaded. But, he turned away and strode down the hall.

After a hot shower, Levi put on his uniform, wrapped his utility belt around his waist, and holstered his gun. Annie was drying a plate when he entered the kitchen. She stopped and gazed at him. He glanced away. He refused to be drawn into her 'little girl lost' eyes.

"Okay. Looks like I'm back on duty. He pulled a card from his pocket and handed it to her. *Dammit. Why did she have to look at him like that? Making him feel like he was deserting her?* "Call the station if you need anything."

Not…call him, but the station. He told himself he wanted nothing more to do with her. He'd be glad when she left for Miami. He strode out the door and didn't look back. If he did, he knew he'd turn right around and make her come with him. Hell if he knew why.

*That's right buddy. You keep telling yourself that.*

# Chapter Eighteen

Less than twenty-four hours after the storm, electricity was restored and cell coverage resumed.

After cleaning the house and readying the place for Liddy and Mark's return, Annie sat in front of the TV eating a sandwich. She bit into the tuna salad on whole wheat and thought about the past few days. It was wonderful how people came together to work after a disaster. Levi had sent in a clean-up crew and a repairman, who was still working on the outside of the house.

After lunch, Annie checked the house one last time for any personal belongings. Her phone rang just as she flipped off the light.

"Hello."

"Anna. Thank God. I've been worried sick about you," Annie's agent, Liz Connors, gushed dramatically.

"Oh, Liz! I can't tell you how wonderful it is to hear a friendly voice."

"So you're all right? You weren't swept away by Cindy?"

"No," she laughed, but why she was laughing was beyond her. There was nothing funny about the past forty-eight hours. "I'm still alive. Although, I imagine some wish I weren't."

"Don't say that. Don't ever say that." The firm reprimand made Annie smile.

"I'm so glad to hear from you," Annie said. "I was thinking about going on to Miami a day early. I don't have to tell you, after my experience here, I'm ready to move on."

"Darling, about Miami. That's why I've been frantic to reach you. They've canceled your shoot."

Annie's stomach plummeted. "What?"

"I'm sorry, honey."

"Are they rescheduling?"

The pause at the other end of the line told Annie all she needed to know.

"With all that's been in the news about you and Alex, the client thinks you could damage their image," Liz said.

"Didn't I tell you this would happen?"

"You did. But frankly, I figured the publicity could only help their overpriced line of clothes. Besides, most people like this salacious stuff. The public usually eats it up."

"Unless they think you're a thief and are responsible for hundreds of people losing their retirement funds. People *hate* that. *I* hate that."

"Honey, there's something else."

Silence hung in the air, thick and suffocating. "What?" The word rushed from her mouth like air from a balloon.

"Banning dropped you from their account."

Banning. Her bread and butter client. She paid most of her bills with her income from them. She'd been their girl, their image for over five years. Their organic skin and hair care products were some of the best in the world.

"How will I live?" She hadn't meant to say that out loud.

"I know, I know. My commission alone paid for my face lift."

"What am I supposed to do now?"

"You need some publicity."

"Publicity? That's what has gotten me in this mess in the first place."

"No. Negative publicity has done that. You need some positive publicity."

Annie groaned.

"Hear me out, Anna. It's time you let the world know about your foundation."

"That's the last thing the world needs to know. They already know I'm involved with it and right now that's enough. After all that's happened, the foundation's investors would pull out if they knew I was the founder and owner. People will stop donating, if they think I have any financial connection to it."

"Yes, but they don't know it's your brain child. Your baby. That it took everything you had to establish it. It's a wonderful story of personal sacrifice. Like No Other has helped hundreds of teenage girls. And with the expansion to small town America, it's only going to get better."

"I don't want the world to know."

"Why?"

"It's personal, Liz." She sucked in a ragged breath. "If people know, they'll want to know details and I'm not interested in sharing that information."

"It's a story of survival. Of overcoming. Plus, you do such wonderful work with those girls. It would show a side of you I'd think you'd want people to know."

"No. I mean it. It's enough they know I'm involved. However long that might be."

"Okay fine. Then, we need to milk your involvement for all it's worth. Since you're scheduled to work with the local girls there, I'll send out a press release alerting the major newspapers as well as TV and radio stations in Florida. The national press is sure to pick up on it."

"Liz, listen—"

"No. You listen. If you don't do something, and I mean soon, your career will be over."

"Fine. But, not this town. Not now. I don't want the focus on me and that's exactly what will happen if you alert the national press. We'll do something big when I'm done here. I promise."

Annie pressed end and continued down the hall with her suitcase in tow. She jammed the Louis Vuitton suitcase in the small trunk and left. She steered the yellow Fiat across the bridge through town and out onto the main highway. Liz meant well, but this was not a good time to be in the public eye. She wanted out of the national spotlight, not in their crosshairs.

She'd decided to get a hotel room while Mark and Liddy's house was being repaired. She could figure out a more permanent place to stay later. Just as she neared the main intersection in town, she spotted a large, rustic RV Trailer Park sign. *Pete's RV Park, 3Miles*. A giant, yellow, arrow pointing left, spanned across the top.

"That sounds interesting." She turned left, and followed the markers. A barrage of potholes met the Fiat like sudden debris from outer space. They were everywhere. Avoiding them proved impossible so she bumped and bobbed along the road until she was nearly sick. The road finally smoothed out as she neared a mass of pine trees and another trailer park sign. This time the arrow pointed right with 0.2 miles to go. After making the turn the pines thickened into a small forest. Annie swallowed and wondered if she'd been mad to consider such an out of the way location. But she trucked on, and finally to her utter delight, she came upon the RV Park.

A selection of vintage recreation vehicles dotted the picture-postcard scene before her. It was like stepping back in time. She parked and got out. The ground was a combination of hard-packed sand and pine needles. Beyond the RVs and the longleaf pines lay a pristine white beach and the sparking Gulf of Mexico. Salt water mingled with a hint of tangy pine, delighting her senses. Behind her and to the right the stately pines created a crescent moon forest around the rest of the perimeter. Someone was playing Michael Buble's, *Home*. It was a fitting song because that was the feeling she got standing in this picturesque trailer park that time forgot. She didn't know if it was because her mother used to talk about her childhood in the 50's but this place seemed familiar to her. It comforted and warmed her heart. Just looking at it gave her a sense of belonging and security and everything she'd longed for as a child. In that instant, Annie knew she could leave New York and live here forever.

"Afternoon." An elderly man, hunching slightly forward at the waist, approached her. "I'm Pete St. John. May I help you?"

"Yes. Hi." Annie shook the man's hand. "Do you rent these?"

"Most of these trailers are private residences but we have a few for rent. Are you interested in a weekly or a monthly rate?"

"I'll be here for about a month."

"Well, camper number two and five are available this week and next. And you can have number seven for as long as you want."

"Okaaay. Why is that?"

"It hasn't been remodeled yet. It's not in bad shape though, and it is clean. Just a bit outdated. I'll show it to you."

As they walked across the sand and pine needle pathway, he told her about the property. "Each unit has all the amenities, of course. Cable TV and Wi-Fi are also included in your rent." He unlocked the door to number 7, then they stepped inside.

It was perfect. Adorable, in fact. The tiny space was compact and seemed to have everything one could ever need. Facing her was a small sink tucked underneath an even smaller window. Above it hung a white and turquoise checked valance. White shelves flanked each side of the window and a compact refrigerator stood to the left of the sink. The table was parallel to the wall on her right with bench seating that turned into a second bed. A single shower and toilet was at the back near the tiny bedroom. Everything was turquoise and white with red vinyl accents.

"It's lovely, Mr. St. John. Why would you ever want to update it? I think it's perfect just the way it is."

"Well, you obviously appreciate the finer things." He chuckled. "But you know how the kids are today. They want HD TV and hot water that doesn't run out after ten minutes."

"The hot water runs out after ten minutes?"

"Not if you conserve it, it doesn't," he added as a matter of fact. "And call me Pete. Nobody calls me Mr. St. John."

"Okay, Pete." She smiled at him. She liked Pete and liked the little trailer. For the next month, it would be home. Her little haven away from the media and its scrutiny. Finally, she could relax.

*Chapter Nineteen*

Three days later, Annie stood on the small stage in Apalacha Key High School's cafeteria waiting for the Friday afternoon press conference and reception to begin. She had wanted to cancel when the school principal informed her the local press had been invited to cover the event. But since she was still using her real name, she relaxed and decided to go with the flow. After all, it was only the local news media. There were only a few reporters standing in front of the small crowd of parents, grandparents, teachers, and teenage girls.

Her foundation, Like No Other, was a well-known and respected charity. Even though it focused on teenage girls from all walks of life, many of them were underprivileged or had been abused or neglected. To cancel because of her own personal concerns would not have been fair to the girls in this small community.

As she gazed across the smiling faces in the room, she noticed the teenage girls tried to dress in the latest fashion and for some it fell flat. Well, that would soon be rectified. Once upon a time, she had been one of these girls. She smiled and looked forward to the session on 'fashion basics'. As a model, it was her favorite topic. Coming from her meager background, she'd learned to copy the latest fashions and trends she'd seen in all of the top magazines. She had some amazing tips on what a complete wardrobe needed and how to build it on a budget.

Amanda Marsh, the school principal, and Eleanor Banks, the school nurse, stood at her side as she prepared to take questions from parents and reporters.

"We are so pleased to have Miss Dell here who is an active participant in Like No Other," Amanda Marsh said. "And speaking for the girls at the high school, they are very excited to have a real fashion model working with them."

"Thank you, Miss Marsh. It's a pleasure to be here and I look forward to working with all of you. Until recently, Like No Other was limited to larger cities. But, about a year ago, the board decided to take the organization to small town America. We couldn't have done it without the active participation from local authorities, community officials, and parents like you. You've been over-whelmingly supportive and the foundation thanks you."

Applause broke from the floor.

"Hi, Meg Townsend, with the Panhandle Post. How long is the program?" she asked.

"It's four weeks. Four Saturdays to be exact. We usually work with the school as to when they want to meet. It can be anywhere from after school to Saturday mornings. Although we also have what we call The LNO Blitz, where someone comes in and holds the four sessions over an entire weekend. It just depends on the community and what works for them. I personally like the four Saturdays. It gives me a chance to really get to know the girls. For me, it's all about the relationship," she answered calmly.

"We've decided to have the sessions on Saturdays," Miss Marsh said. "So those girls who participate in after-school activities can attend."

"Miss Dell, everyone in Apalacha Key want to know something about you. Where are you from and have you always wanted to be a model?"

Annie's mouth went dry. The last thing she wanted was to have to reveal personal information about herself. In the past, most questions dealt only with the charity but small towns, she supposed, were different. They wanted to know you. It was probably too much to expect other-wise.

"I'm…from all over actually. Mainly, the mid-west. " She forced a smile and tried to ignore the flutter in the pit of her stomach. "My family moved a lot while I was growing up." She finished lamely.

Not the most forthright answer, she thought as she eyed the group of reporters, suddenly wishing she were anywhere but here.

"And your interest in modeling?" The female reporter quickly reminded her.

In that moment she thought about her beautiful, dark-haired mother and the red sequined dress she used to wear. She could still see her laughing eyes as she twirled, making the dress flair around her knees. It had been a happy moment for the two of them, until her father walked in the room. The image faded and she swallowed.

"I got my interest in modeling and fashion from my mother." She didn't want to talk about her mother. Not with strangers.

A sandy-haired man near the back of the room raised his pen. She nodded to him and waited.

"Ethan Knight with the *Orlando Times*."

Annie hesitated. Orlando? She sucked in a deep breath. What was someone from Orlando doing here? She glanced at Miss Marsh, surprised to see her face had lost most of its color. Any other time, she would have given more thought to the school principal's odd reaction, but right now Annie had to pull herself together.

She blinked and focused on the reporter.

"Miss Dell," he continued, "what do you know about the recent scandal concerning Alex Langdon and Like No Other?"

Annie almost choked. What in the world was he talking about? What had Alex done? She scanned the room while her mind scrambled for an answer. Her gaze fell on the tall sheriff leaning against the wall at the back of the cafeteria. For a brief moment, her eyes locked with his, then she looked back at the reporter.

"I don't know anything about that. Where did you hear that, if I may ask?"

"Late last night. It came across the Associated Press. There's speculation he may have used the organization to launder money. It's been in the news all morning."

"I'm afraid I haven't watched the news for days now, with the recent hurricane and all."

"Are you concerned how this might affect the charity?" the reporter from the Panhandle Post asked.

"Well, of course. But as I don't know any of the details —"

"I understand the founder of Like No Other chooses to be anonymous. Do you have any knowledge as to who this person might be?"

"I have no idea," she lied.

"Are you comfortable working for a charitable foundation that's linked to the Alex Langdon scandal?" asked another.

"Don't you find the link to Alex Langdon suspicious?"

"After all, thousands of dollars have been donated," chimed in another.

Annie raised her hand to still the questions. "Please, I can't answer these questions, but let me tell you what I do know. Like No Other is a well-known and respected charity. In spite of the Alex Langdons of this world. For the past five years this organization has helped countless teenage girls, from all walks of life, overcome self-image issues. As you know, some of these teens were abused and neglected. As a volunteer, I have been privileged to be involved with this organization from the beginning and until this moment, I personally have never seen any abuse of funds. Keep in mind, each community has a local mentor *and* treasurer. Any money you raise stays right here." She pointed firmly to the stage floor with sharp staccato jabs. "These next few Saturdays are about these young women. And I for one don't want to see anything damage that." She sucked in a sharp breath. "Any other questions," she asked and gazed out over the crowd of faces in hopes of ending this discussion. "No? Then may I suggest we get on with the reception?" She forced a smile and looked to Miss Marsh for confirmation.

"Brilliant idea. Let's give a hand to Miss Annie Dell."

Applause broke from the cafeteria floor. With her heart in her throat, Annie waved 'thank you' to the crowd, then left the stage. Normally, this would have been her favorite part, meeting the parents and the girls. But she was sick inside. What had Alex done to her charity? She painted on her *Family Circle* magazine smile and counted the minutes until she could escape.

# Chapter Twenty

Levi continued to lean against the wall, watching her. One second she was all cool, calm and collected, and the next, agitated and pinning her pleading gaze in his direction. As if he could do anything about it.

She exited the stage and immediately regained composure as three teenage girls surrounded her. Back to her glamorous self. And man could she work a room. He watched her smile and greet parents and their teen daughters like she owned the place. Hard to believe this was the same person who stumbled through the last several minutes with reporters. Under different circumstances, she probably did a great job with them.

It pained him to watch her fumble and stutter when asked personal questions. He shook his head. Hard to side step when a hundred pairs of eyes watched you. But when asked about Like No Other, her words sprang from her lips like a well-oiled machine. It was obvious she loved this organization and was proud of the work they did.

Town officials, local business owners, parents and reporters flocked to her side. He wasn't surprised. There was something about her that certainly attracted attention. Bees to honey and all that. He hated to admit it, but hell if he didn't also like honey. He'd fought it hard enough but she still got under his skin.

As he watched her, he wondered if Like No Other would continue to allow her to work with them, considering her connection to Alex Langdon and his alleged connection to LNO. He guessed it wouldn't be long before the foundation terminated her involvement with them. Yup. Only a matter of time.

He folded his arms across his chest and watched two girls with their fathers shake hands with Annie. The two men were smiling and laughing at something Annie had said, while the girls stood next to Annie for a photo. He grunted. You'd think she'd want to disappear after all the negative attention in New York. Then he realized she had disappeared, different name and all.

Even though there was still a lot of clean up from Cindy yet to be done, that hadn't kept him from looking into her boyfriend's criminal activity. Alex Langdon was a piece of work. Charged with three counts of fraud and one count of theft. How could she live with the guy and not know something was up?

He pushed himself away from the block wall and made his way across the crowded room. She was now talking to three teenage girls. Annie's eyes sparkled as she clasped each girl's hand in turn, her beautiful smile contagious, demanding a ready response from everyone around her. But then she noticed him and stilled in mid-sentence. Her eyes blinked a few times, before turning back to the girls to dismiss them. After they walked away, she turned wide, honey-gold eyes on him and waited.

As he neared her, pure sunshine filled his senses. She smelled just like the day he'd found her in the car terrified to cross the bridge. At the time he couldn't place the smell but it now came to him in a flash. Lemon groves in central Florida. That was it. She smelled like sweet lemon blossoms.

Her pretty mouth turned down at the corners.

"I'm surprised to see you here. Or, did you come just to torment me?" The bite in her tone completely made null and void any reference to lemons, fresh squeezed or otherwise.

He stopped in front of her, stuffed his hands in his pockets and leaned forward from his waist. "I bet you're glad that's over."

Expecting to see daggers at his comment, he pulled himself up short at the expression that covered her face. Her sleek, fashionable, model body said poised and in control, but her expressive eyes were nothing short of a distress call.

"Cheer up. I've seen worse press conferences. You actually didn't do too badly, until you couldn't remember where you were from."

"I'm sorry. Did you want something?" She raised her small powdered chin, which further accentuated her disturbed countenance. Even though her eyes glistened a challenge he was more than up for, all the blustering in the world couldn't hide her underlying distress.

"You know for a moment back there, I thought you might be asking for my help."

"And what moment was that?" she snapped.

He smiled down at her. "When your eyes latched onto mine and cried, *help!*"

She pursed her lips and looked away just as Miss Marsh came up to them.

* * *

"Hello, Sheriff."

"Amanda."

"It's a wonderful turnout, isn't it?" Miss Marsh said. "Looks like everyone here is enjoying themselves. Annie,

I can't thank you enough for taking time from your busy schedule to work with us. The girls are thrilled and can't wait for Saturday."

"Thank you, Miss Marsh," she said. "I'm excited about it, too."

"Please, call me Amanda." She grasped Annie's hand. "Well, I have to get back to work. I'm sure you two will enjoy working together over the next several weeks."

"What do you mean?" Annie asked, looking from one to the other.

"Oh, I'm, sorry. I thought you knew. Sheriff Hawke is Like No Other's honorary chairman." Amanda smiled, then left.

Annie's jaw dropped and her head whipped around to stare at him.

"You know, it's all I can do not to place my hand under your chin and shut your lovely mouth."

She clamped her mouth shut and folded her arms across her chest.

"Have I told you how beautifully your eyes darken when you're angry?" he said.

She rolled her eyes and huffed. "Why am I not surprised."

"By the way, to answer your earlier question, that's why I'm here. And, I'm so looking forward to our time together."

She eyed him with all the venom she could conjure and could tell by the smug look on his face that her venom held no sting.

"Don't tell me you weren't aware of that part of the organization?"

Of course she was aware. It had been her brainchild. To get a local civil servant to be honorary chairperson of the charity would insure community involvement as well as local participation. What local government wouldn't want such a positive influence on the young girls in their community? The board had loved her suggestion and followed up with a national campaign rallying local law enforcement officers and congressional leaders to participate.

"Of course, I knew that. I just didn't know it was you." She took a step back.

He glanced around the room. "You know, in light of recent events, I'm surprised you're still here. Do you think it's wise to bring this kind of attention to yourself?"

"This has been scheduled for several months now. Liddy set it up for me. Besides, it's only a local thing. I can't imagine my being here will get that much attention."

"Don't count on it. Somebody's bound to recognize you, fake name or not. What happened to Miami?"

"Miami got cancelled, so Miss Marsh—Amanda—and I moved up the event. And as for my personal schedule, well, it's personal and no concern of yours." She glanced up at him to find his mocking gaze on her.

"I made it my concern when I discovered your connection to Alex Langdon. Speaking of which…"

"I have no interest in discussing him with you or anyone else."

* * *

"Come on. Don't you think it's unusual that Like No Other is suddenly linked with him?"

She shrugged and began to stroll around the room but not before he saw the distress back in her eyes. He walked along side of her.

"So you have nothing to say?" He peered down at her lovely profile wishing she would trust him, but when she didn't answer, he continued. "Well, let me give it a try and see if I have this straight. Oh, and feel free to stop and correct me at any point. You volunteer for Like No Other, you dated Alex Langdon and now Alex is under investigation for allegedly using that organization for his own underhanded and illegal purposes. Do I have that right, so far?"

She stopped and spun toward him. "Are you accusing me of something? If so spit it out." Her chest heaved and her topaz eyes lit up with angry sparks.

"Don't you find that odd? I find that extremely odd. Even you have to admit the connection is pretty fantastic. I'd just like some answers, that's all. As local chairman, I can't have the community donating funds to an organization that's compromised and possibly illegal."

She blew out a frustrated breath, turned her back on him and commenced to stroll around the room.

"I'm not connected to him." She gripped her hands tightly in front of her. "At least, not in the way you think."

"And which way is that?" he asked.

She stopped and looked pointedly up at him. "That I'm involved with his dishonest actions, that I'm a liar and a thief."

She was trembling and obviously shaken. It was clear this conversation had upset her. Cupping her elbow, he deftly guided her around a group of parents, discouraging any opportunity for her to stop and chat. He wanted her full attention.

"Then what is your connection?"

"You mean you haven't found out through your own investigation?"

"This is my own investigation. Eyewitness accounts are an important part of any investigation. Especially criminal." He paused to let that sink in. "Well?"

Her eyes dropped to somewhere around his third shirt button.

"It's personal."

"How personal?"

She bit her lip and a frown creased her pretty brow. He fought the urge to smooth it away with his thumb.

"Was it because of his money? Is that what attracted you?"

Her eyes flew up to meet his. Large, brown, honey pots, he knew if given half the chance, could easily melt his heart.

"Yes." She barely said the word but something slammed into his inner region as if she'd screamed it. Well, at least she was truthful enough to admit it.

He nodded. "I see you're still not using your real name. As the sheriff, I feel it's my duty to inform Amanda—"

Annie turned white. Any tan she'd gotten over the past couple of weeks disappeared. "You can't tell her. If you do, the only people to lose out will be these girls." She clamped her teeth on her lower lip and stared up at him. Her eyes filled with unshed tears.

Oh hell! What was it about her that made him feel like he was back in high school? He was thirty-two for crying out loud.

He glanced around the room. All he needed was for someone to see that 'old ironsides' made the pretty little newcomer cry. He'd have hell to pay from more than one quarter. It wouldn't be the first time he'd be taken to task for being too tough with the opposite sex. Thank God Liddy wasn't in town.

He reclaimed Annie's elbow and guided her over to the punch table, thankful she didn't resist. "For someone who's supposed to be so tough, you sure do cry a lot." He filled a cup with the sweet pink mixture and handed it to her. He watched her take a sip hopeful the action would give her a chance to compose herself. "Okay. I won't say anything."

Her golden brown eyes gazed up at him as if he'd just thrown her a life preserver.

"But, I'm not sure I'm doing you any favors, and if you're innocent, does it really matter?"

"What matters is what she believes. Take you for instance. I've told you the truth but you're still suspicious of me. I have no idea how she'll react if she finds out."

"The worst thing that could happen is that she'd fire you and ask the foundation to send someone else. Or, she may not do anything. I know Amanda Marsh. She's a reasonable person and fair minded."

"Most people are until you give them a reason not to trust you." She brushed a wayward strand of hair from her forehead. "Then they think the worst."

She sighed and glanced across the room at a small group that had gathered near the cookie table. They were sipping on punch and giggling about something.

"You see those girls over there?"

"Yes." He folded his arms across his chest.

"What do you know about them? I mean really know? They look happy enough, right? But, what happens to them when they go home? Who greets them at the door? How are they greeted? With a hug and a snack and questions about the quiz they had in math that morning? Or, by a suspicious monster."

He blinked and stared at her. *Where the hell did that come from?*

Her eyes had become hard and cold and she suddenly had his undivided attention.

"What's your point?" he asked.

"I know who they are and how they think. About themselves, about others." She laid her hand on his forearm. "I know what worries them. I know they constantly compare themselves to everyone around them. Even the "cool" girls don't believe they are." Annie raised pleading eyes to his. "Please, don't ruin this. I want to work with them. With everything that's been going on, I haven't had a chance to in a long time. Plus, I…I need to hide. For just a while longer. Until this mess with Alex blows over."

She gazed up at him with such mute appeal it was all he could do not to take her in his arms. All he'd thought about since the hurricane was her in his arms. It had been sheer heaven.

He softened toward her. "Life isn't perfect, as much as you'd like for it to be."

"You think I don't know that?"

He looked down at her serious upturned face. "All right. I won't say anything…Miss Dell."

"Thank you. And if it makes you feel any better, that is my real name. So, you see, you're not really deceiving anyone."

"Time will tell."

Annie tugged on the hem of her silky white blouse and threw her shoulders back. "Now, if you're through, I'm here to mingle with the guests."

"One more thing." Annie stopped and turned back to him. "What if someone recognizes you? Like that guy from the *Orlando Times*."

"I didn't want any press here. That was Amanda's idea. Although she seemed pretty disturbed at his presence."

"A moot point at this juncture." He shoved his hands in his pockets. "Don't think for a minute he's done asking you questions. That he won't be digging into your identity as soon as he's back at his office. I've read his editorials and I can assure you, your evasive answers only whet his appetite. If I were you, I'd get prepared for some backlash."

"Watch out. You sound like you want to protect me," she said.

"I don't want my town linked to scandal, that's all. But you're right. My job is to protect and serve and I plan to protect my community and you, if you'll let me. That reporter has been eyeing you for the past thirty minutes. Chomping at the bit, so I'd get ready if I were you. I suppose you'll have a lie prepared for him, too."

"Is it so wrong to want to protect myself?"

"No. But there are other ways to accomplish that. Ways that don't require lying. But the fact that you seem to resort to that, tells me a great deal about you."

She glanced at the glass in her hand, then back at him. "Not everyone is perfect like you, Sheriff Hawke."

"Trust me, I'm far from perfect, *Miss* Dell." He gave her a brief nod and walked away.

* * *

Suddenly, she was thirteen years old and standing before her father. He wore a uniform with a star, too. Except his was blue. Even after all these years, the image of him standing over her in a rage still made it difficult for her to breathe. Yes, she was good liar. She'd had to be, to survive.

# Chapter Twenty-One

Levi pushed through the gym doors and strode to his patrol car. That woman could needle her way under the skin of a dinosaur. He rubbed his hand across the back of his neck. Her honey gold eyes lingered and made him think all kinds of things that would be highly inappropriate, especially while on duty.

Once inside, he checked for messages, then drove the few short blocks to the station.

Minutes later, he was seated at his desk and logging into his computer. Maybe it was time he did a little checking on Miss Anna Delany. He'd search for anything on Annie Dell, as well. It was only a gut reaction but something else was worrying her. Was she ashamed of something in her past? Had she done something illegal?

The page in front of him loaded and he typed in, *Anna Delany* to see where that would lead. Not much. At least not to anything new and that wasn't already all over the news. Basic information about her modeling career, her driver's license, her three-year relationship with Langdon but nothing else. The trail ended. Odd. It was as if she never existed before 2005.

Next he typed in *Annie Dell.* After he followed more prompts and filled in more information he finally hit something. He paused, sat back in his chair and stared at the screen. The face staring back at him was Annie all right. She was a lot younger but it was definitely her. It was an Amber Alert for one fifteen-year-old teenage girl named Anna Marie Dell. Last seen in Rockford, Iowa on August 10, 2005.

Even as a teenager she was a beauty. He placed his elbows on the desk and continued to read. As he delved further into the document he discovered she was a runaway, and that her father was a cop. According to him, she had been a handful since her mother had died. Always lying and in and out of trouble at school.

Levi chewed the inside of his lip and read to the end of the document. She had never been found.

He leaned back in his chair. So she'd changed her name, insuring she'd never be found. But there was something else bothering him. Her father's statement. It didn't ring true. Not only his tone, but also the wording. How could he have known that she wasn't kidnapped or worse? In fact, he was accusatory. Like he was happy to be rid of her. Odd behavior for a father who was supposed to be concerned for his daughter.

Good Lord above. He raised his hand to his head and thought about the night of the hurricane. Her reaction to his handcuffing her, her fear of storms and what she'd said earlier, 'greeted by a monster.' Could her father have abused her? He looked back at the school photo of the fifteen-year-old Annie. The shy smile peeked from the screen with more uncertainty than happiness. As if she wasn't sure she had any right to that feeling. They say the eyes are the mirror to one's soul. If that was true, then Annie Dell had been miserable.

He steepled his fingers and rested his mouth on his hands. No kid runs away for nothing and deliberately stays lost for ten years.

He quickly jotted down the name, Frank Dell, to look up later. Right now he had to go back out on patrol.

He walked down the hall and out the door. *What did he do to you, Annie? Or, were you simply just that much trouble?* He could almost bring himself to believe it, if his own recent experience with her was anything to go by. But, he couldn't shake the shy, uncertain expression of the young Annie staring back at him from the computer screen. Haunting him with every step he took.

* * *

Annie pulled the mini coupe in front of the pink and white trailer and cut the ignition. She'd rented the car from Enterprise the day after she'd found the RV Park. The extra legroom was a nice change after Liddy's Fiat.

Pete was at her neighbor's place sitting at a picnic table drinking coffee. She got out of the car, waved, and hurried inside. This was not a good time to engage in conversation. Pulling the aluminum and glass door closed, she flipped on the lights, set her bag on the vinyl sofa, then turned on the TV. It was just as Ethan Knight had said. Alex Langdon and his connection to Like No Other were all over the news.

Annie sat down with a thud and covered her mouth with her hand. This simply could not be happening. Could her life get any worse? She jumped up and switched off the TV. What she needed was some fresh air. In New York, she frequently took long walks in Central Park. She enjoyed nature and the walks offered the double bonus of burning calories and clearing the mind.

Moments later, after changing into white shorts, a blue t-shirt and sneakers she walked across the dried pine needles that graced the RV Park grounds. Even though it was near dinnertime, there was still plenty of daylight left to take a nice stroll in the wooded area.

Pine trees loomed tall and straight into the early evening sky and the sun casts its iridescent glow over the tops of the trees. It was beautiful. Serene. She grew calmer with each step she took. The fragrant sent of pine filled the air and infused her entire body. Naturally fragrant. Not like the chemicals some companies used in their products. This was heady and delicious, reminding her of Christmas. Her mother had loved to bake and Annie imagined her mom in their little kitchen in Iowa. She could almost smell the sugary cinnamon and apples. It was funny how one smell could release a flood of memories. Some good. Some bad, and some very bad.

She slapped her hand around the nearest tree trunk and leveraged herself over a large limb, her bare legs slightly brushing over the dried prickly needles. Stepping gingerly over the jutting branch she cleared the prickly mass and continued forward.

She hated that Levi thought of her as a liar. Saddened her, really. Sure, she'd deliberately been a thorn in his side but that was before the hurricane. Since that night, so much had changed for her. She was terribly attracted to him and it wasn't only because of his amazing good looks. Even though he was hardnosed and unbending, he was the most comforting person she'd been around in years. His authoritative presence and his habit of taking control of a situation should have irritated her, but it didn't. It fit him. She shrugged and kept walking. He'd probably laugh if he knew, but Levi Hawke made her feel safe. When he held her during the hurricane she, along with her terror, had melted in his arms. He was a rock. A shield. A hiding place. And for someone coming from an abused background, that was saying something.

She closed her eyes, frustrated with her silly mental ramblings. These sappy feelings weren't real, but were simply reaction to having a less than ideal childhood.

She continued to meander through the woods and until this moment hadn't realized how dark it had gotten. She stopped. It was so quiet it was almost creepy. She turned around in her spot, completely surrounded by pine trees. Dusk was upon her and there wasn't a light in sight. She quickly walked back the way she'd come. At least she thought this was the way. She stopped again, rubbed her fingers nervously back and forth across her chin and looked around her. Which way was the park? Maybe if she focused on listening, she'd hear something. Voices. Anything.

Nothing.

Not even a cricket.

*Okay. This is not the worst thing that's ever happened to you.* She pushed away the fact that she hadn't brought her cell phone or a flashlight with her. To still the oncoming panic, she swallowed against the dryness in her mouth and focused on the sunset. When she'd started out the sun had been behind her.

"That means I should be walking…that way." She turned, then pointed her finger toward the sun. Making sure the setting sun faced her, she proceeded to walk in that direction.

Her breaths quickened with each step, more out of fear than fatigue. If Anna Delany was anything, she was in shape. Like a deer, she bounded through the forest, the sound of dried leaves, pine needles, and pinecones crunching under her feet. Panting, she quickly moved forward until she was jogging. She stumbled, righted herself, and kept going until it was too dark to see.

She stopped, placed her hands on her hips, and sucked in a ragged breath. Gasping, she bent forward at her waist, then pulled herself upright to lean against a tree trunk. She cupped her hands around her mouth and yelled. "Hello! Can anyone hear me?" She stood silent and listening, but still nothing. How could she have gotten this far from the park? She rested her head against the tree. She was most definitely in trouble.

# Chapter Twenty-Two

Levi pulled his patrol car off the road to a secluded spot, then alerted dispatch to his location. It was the only low point on this stretch of road. He re-positioned his radar gun, unscrewed the top of his coffee thermos and waited. This stretch of road was practically deserted, just far enough outside of Apalacha Key that traffic was nil. The small fishing town nestled in the curve of the Florida panhandle was perfect for the calmer life he'd chosen as a peace officer. He paused with the cup to his lips. *That is until lately.* The image of glistening brown eyes were never far from his thoughts.

He sighed, sipped his coffee and waited. In the past hour, he'd already pulled over three drivers, a family in a Tahoe, a single male in a Corvette, and a middle-aged woman in a white Ford F-150. He was ready for this shift and all the excuses for speeding to end.

Today was supposed to be his day off but Davidson had called in with the flu and Levi had to fill in at the last minute.

He checked his watch. Seven-thirty. He tossed the empty thermos on the passenger seat and started the engine. Just as he was about to make his way home a call came in from dispatch.

"We need an officer near your location. A resident has gone missing at Pete's RV Park."

"Okay, I'm on it," Levi responded then replaced the radio.

Levi spotted Pete St. John and a couple of other men in front of one of the trailers and pulled to a stop.

"That was quick, Sheriff."

"I was in the neighborhood." He shook Pete's hand and nodded to the other two men who appeared to be a father and teenage son. "What happened?"

"My new resident, Annie Dell, went for a walk in the woods and hasn't come back."

"When did she leave?"

"Around six or so. It was before dark."

"What was she wearing?" He looked pointedly at Pete waiting for an answer.

"White shorts and a blue t-shirt." The teenage boy piped up, happy to give Levi the details.

"Anything else?"

"She was wearing Nike's and her hair was down. You know, not pulled back or anything."

Levi gave him a brief smile. "Okay. Good."

Pete handed him a thermos. "Hot coffee. She may need it when you find her."

"Thanks." Levi put the thermos in his backpack between the night vision goggles and the fleece blanket.

"I'll call for backup if I need any help. If she comes out before I find her, call me on this." He handed Pete a walkie-talkie.

Pete nodded. "Will do."

Levi turned on his flashlight and scanned the woods in front of him. He pointed the beam of light first left, then to the right, scanning the terrain as he moved forward. Autumn was beautiful on the panhandle. Warm, sunny days and cool nights. He thought about Annie wearing only shorts and a t-shirt. She was probably cold right about now.

A sudden movement caught his eye. He paused, pointed the light to investigate but saw nothing. He walked and scanned for about twenty minutes. "Anneeee!"

He placed one foot in front of the other, constantly scanning the area. "Anneeee!"

"Over here!"

It was faint but it was her voice. "Annie, keep calling to me!"

"I'm over here! I'm here!"

He moved quickly toward the sound of her voice, keeping the light in front of him. Then he saw her. She was sitting on the ground with a large Pine tree at her back. She raised her hand over her face to block the beam of light.

"Thank goodness," she said, teeth chattering.

He slid the backpack off, then got down on his haunches in front of her. "Are you all right? Are you hurt?"

"I sprained my ankle. I don't think it's too bad, but when I try to stand it hurts like heck."

He splayed the light on her ankle, assessing the injury. It was already twice the normal size. "Yeah, I'd say you did a good job of it." He secured the flashlight on the ground next to them. "It's pretty swollen." He pulled out the fleece, draped it over her shoulders, and wrapped it snugly in front of her. She was shivering from head to toe. He placed his hands on her bare arms, applying brisk up and down movements to warm her flesh. "How's that? Better?"

"Yeah. Thanks."

She clutched the blanket to her chest while he unscrewed the top of the coffee thermos. "Here, this should help, too," he said.

She cradled her hands around the cup and took a sip.

"Take a minute and warm up, then I'll get you home."

He dropped his gaze from her glistening eyes, angled the flashlight toward the lower half of her body, then gave his full attention to her injury.

"Okay, I'm going to touch your ankle. Let me know if I hurt you."

"Don't worry, I will."

Something about her tone made him glance at her. Even the night shadows couldn't conceal her pinched and drawn features. She was obviously prepared for the worst. He scooted back and gently lifted her right foot.

She sucked in a sharp breath. "Careful."

"Sorry."

Her shoulders were raised and she held herself rigid, hugging the coffee to her chest. He peeled the cup from her fingers, tossed out the remainder of hot liquid, and placed the cup and the thermos back in the knapsack.

"I'm going to help you stand. Okay?"

She clamped her teeth over her lip and nodded.

"Just put your weight on your left foot and lean into me." In one movement, he had her up and standing with his arm secured around her waist. She winced and leaned into him.

"Are we good?"

"I think so." She sounded breathless.

"Here's how this works. I'm going to lift you off the ground while you hop beside me." With her tucked against his side, he lifted her and took a step forward, then another.

"Owe. Owe. Wait. Stop." She clutched his waist. "That really hurts."

"All right, let's try piggy back." He got down on one knee and waited for her to climb on. Annie placed one hand on his shoulder, lifted her sprained foot, then straddled his back.

"Good. Don't move. When I stand up I'll grab your other leg. Hopefully, it won't hurt too much."

"I'm sorry to be such a wuss."

"You're not a wuss. You're doing great." Levi slid his arms under both her knees, then stood. "Comfy?"

"Perfectly," she chuckled halfheartedly.

"Good girl. Let's go."

* * *

Annie wrapped her arms around Levi's neck and held tight. His back felt wonderful. Solid and deliciously warm and under different circumstances, she'd be sighing right now instead of moaning. With each jarring step he took, sharp knife-like jabs shot through her flesh. She clenched her teeth against the pain.

He stumbled. She cried out, whimpered, and pressed her face into his back.

He stopped. "You okay back there?"

"Yeah, it hurts, that's all." She took a deep cleansing breath, hoping it would temper the pain, but her ankle still throbbed.

Levi unhooked the flashlight from his waist, flicked it on, and handed it to her. "Here. I need more light. We're almost there."

Ten minutes later they broke from the trees into the RV Park. The glowing porch lights from the trailers were a welcome sight.

Pete was waiting and when he saw them, ran to her trailer and opened the door.

Once inside, Levi carefully slid her off his back onto the small vinyl sofa. He placed his arms underneath her hips and legs, then swiveled her bottom until her feet were up on the seat. She gripped her leg right above the knee and squeezed, hoping the action would somehow stop the shooting pain.

Levi's expression was intense but thoughtful and the look of concern on his face warmed her insides. He'd been great tonight. She couldn't think of a time when a man was ever this gentle or caring toward her. *Don't get used to it. He's only doing his duty.*

"There's ibuprofen in the cabinet above the sink," she said.

Pete was on it while Levi gently unlaced her sneaker. "Hold on Pete, I've got something stronger in my bag."

Pete found the brown medicine bottle in the knapsack, then fixed her a glass of water.

Annie dutifully swallowed the pill. "Thank you Pete."

"Let's get your shoe off." Levi cupped his large hand underneath her calf.

Planting her fists on the seat near her hips, she braced herself. Levi unlaced her sneaker then slipped it gingerly from her foot. Next came the sock, which was much easier on her nerve endings. He lowered her foot and turned to Pete.

"You can go. Thanks so much," Levi said.

"Does she need to go to the emergency room?"

"No, she's fine."

Was he kidding? How did he know if she was fine? For a long second she glared at Levi, but since he refused to look her way, she pursed her lips and nodded at Pete. "Thanks for your help." She gave Pete a pitiful wave.

"I'm just glad you're okay." He nodded to Levi and left.

"And so goes another minion…summarily dismissed. Is that how you treat everybody?" She was completely exasperated.

Levi stood to his full six foot two inch height, his mouth set in annoyance and laid his hawk-eyed stare on her.

"Sorry," she said. "But I'm so over that look. If you're trying to intimidate me, you can stop." *But can I help it if the earth moves every time I'm near you. I've cried in your arms. Nestled in your wonderful embrace and clung to your broad masculine back a mere hour ago. No. You don't intimidate me, Mr. Sheriff. You just rock my world.*

He continued to stare down at her, giving a look that plainly said she was an insect to be squashed.

"Would you like me to leave?" he asked.

She pressed her lips together. "Not really."

"I appreciate your concern for Pete's feelings. But you obviously missed the relief on his face when I told him he could go. He's been waiting here for two hours and he has to get up early. I know Pete. He'd still be here hovering in the background if I hadn't said anything and there was nothing more he could do."

Annie lay back against a pillow and watched Levi yank open the freezer door. "How do you know I'm fine, by the way? Maybe I'm not fine," she blurted out. "This hurts like the devil."

"I know it hurts but I've seen my fair share of injuries and this one's not that bad. You just need to apply some heat and cold compresses to your ankle. Where are your plastic bags?" His facial expression was back to that no nonsense, all officer of the law, business.

"In the basket on the top shelf," she snapped.

After filling the bag with ice, he sat back down on the edge of the couch next to her and held it on her swollen ankle. On first contact, the icy bag stung her flesh, but soon numbed the area, easing the pain.

"This should get the swelling down. Afterwards, we'll apply some heat."

"How? I don't have a heating pad or anything."

"Don't worry. I'll figure it out."

"Are you always this smug?"

He arched a masculine brow in her direction. "I see the pain killer has kicked in. You were whimpering only minutes ago."

"I was not."

He smiled and her heart skipped a beat.

"My ankle's starting to burn." She leaned forward and grabbed her leg just above her ankle. "Sheesh."

Levi lifted her hand and placed it over the bag. "Hold that in place while I get the heat ready." He stood to his feet and glanced at her before he walked over to the sink.

He grabbed a hand towel and proceeded to heat it under the hot water tap.

He rung it out, stepped back to the couch, then replaced the icepack with the hot towel.

She sucked a long slurp of air through her lips.

"Too hot?"

"A bit."

"Hold that in place while I replenish the ice."

Her eyes followed him to the fridge. He was wearing jeans and a kaki shirt, and his badge and Glock were clipped to his waist. As if he could feel her scrutiny, he glanced back at her, unclipped his gun, then laid it on the Formica table.

She rolled her eyes. "Afraid I'll go for it?"

He grinned and reached in the freezer for more ice. "If you did," he nodded at her ankle, "at least I wouldn't have to cuff you this time." He filled the bag, opened the fridge, and pulled out two Cokes. "Would you like one?"

"Sure."

He unscrewed the caps and handed her one of the bottles. When she took it, her fingers brushed his. They were warm and strong and she wondered how it would feel to hold his hand.

She took a long swig. "You know, I heard Coca Cola filled the last glass bottle of coke earlier this year and somebody paid thousands of dollars for the very last bottle that come off the line."

He shook his head. "That's crazy."

"I know. People give value to the strangest things." She held the bottle higher and looked underneath, then took another swig. "I hardly ever drink these. If my agent could see me, she'd freak."

"Your world sounds a bit suffocating. How do you live like that every day?"

"Self-discipline. Something you also know a lot about." She raised her coke bottle to him in a mock toast.

"How so?"

"Really. You don't know?"

The corner of his mouth tilted upward. "I'm just curious to see what your answer is. So tell me."

"Well, let's see. For starters, you have rock hard abs. A sure sign you work out."

"And how would you know that? Just because I've had my shirt off in front of you…"

"And your pants," she couldn't resist reminding him.

He clamped his lips together and shook his head.

She laughed. "You're so easily irritated. You really need to learn to lighten up, Sheriff."

"Yup, I'd say that medicine has finally kicked in."

"Don't change the subject. We were talking about your self-discipline. Trust me. Any guy with arms like yours and with your strength…well, enough said." She smiled up at him. "Plus, you held me in your arms and a girl can tell a lot about a man when he holds her in his arms."

* * *

Levi gazed down at her and bit back a smile. The powerful painkiller had taken effect and she was suddenly all soft and dreamy eyed and loose tongued. His heart thudded in his chest.

"All right," he said. "I'll take your word for it. And, confirm what you say is true. What else?" He took a pull on his coke and watched her. Even with dirt and grime splattered across her cheek and forehead, she was beautiful.

"Hum, let's see," she said. "Aside from the many times you kept yourself from wringing my lovely neck, you displayed nothing but utter and complete and I'm certain newsworthy self-control."

"You think your neck is lovely?" He brushed his hand across his mouth and watched her.

"No. But, *Harper's Bazaar* certainly does." She grinned sheepishly and stretched like a kitten. "The Ribbed Leaf Neck Gown, by Alexander McQueen, sets off her lovely neck to perfection," she quoted, then giggled. "And for three-thousand dollars, it sure should."

He could believe it. Her neck was lovely as well as the rest of her. Her slender arms, her small waist and her long toned legs stirred up a raw ache deep within his gut.

"And last and most importantly," she added. "You're non-emotional."

His thudding heart paused and slowed to a steady rhythm and something inside him cringed at her honest, forthright description. He thought about the day his sister died. Yes, he was non-emotional. It was the perfect defense against the pain. But, since meeting Annie, the last thing he was, especially in regards to her, was non-emotional. She'd made him come back to the real world with all of its pleasures and pain. She had no idea what she did to him just by her very existence. She'd turned his orderly, no nonsense life upside down in more ways than he cared to admit.

"Like Robo Cop," she said, interrupting his musing. "You do know Hollywood is making a new movie about him, right?"

He shook his head. "No, I hadn't heard."

"You." She jabbed a slender finger to his chest. "Could star in it." She lifted her finger, then placed her soft hand against his cheek. He watched her study his face and wondered what she was thinking. "You're certainly handsome enough."

Her golden eyes glistened and her lips called to him like Odysseus' sirens. The desire to kiss her rushed through him like the blood in his veins. Pounding over and over in his brain. *Kiss her. Kiss her.*

Instead, he stood, snatched the lukewarm towel from her ankle, then replaced it with the ice pack. "Hold that for a second." He didn't wait for her reply but strode to the sink to run warm water over the clammy cloth. After he squeezed out the excess, he walked back and sat down on the edge of the couch near her waist.

"What are you doing?" She gazed at him with a wary expression in her eyes.

"Cleaning your face. It's a mess."

"Oh."

"Hold still." He gently wiped her forehead and cheek. "There you go." He plucked a dried leaf from her hair. "All cleaned up."

A crease formed between her eyes. "You're a strange duck."

"Well that's one I haven't heard."

"No really. You confuse me, Sheriff Hawke."

"How so?"

She tipped the coke bottle up and took the last swig. "Oh, I don't know. One minute you're scolding and the next you're kind of sweet." She gazed up at him. "I thought I had you all figured out, then you go and do something like hang around to put heat and ice on my ankle. You and I both know you didn't have to stay here and do that."

Her eyelids fluttered and she sank back against the sofa. "You know what I think?"

He shook his head and eyed her.

"I think deep down, you're a sweet guy."

Her lids drooped then fluttered open and she gazed up at him with those golden sleepy eyes of hers.

A smile tugged at the corners of his mouth and he wondered if he'd given her too strong of a dose. Her childlike adoration touched him but there was absolutely nothing childlike about the way she looked at that moment. For one thing, that blue t-shirt clung to her perfect figure, drawing attention to the rise and fall of her breasts.

"No one is ever sweet to me." She added dreamily. "No man, that is."

Her sorrowful puppy eyes touched him.

"But, you. You're different. You march to your own drum. You don't care what anyone thinks. I respect that."

"Thank you," he said.

"How come you came to my rescue tonight?" She yawned. "Why not another deputy?"

"I was in the area. I was the closest. Plain and simple. If one of my other deputies had been in the area, they would have answered the call."

"So. You were just doing your duty. Nothing more." She glanced away from him. She seemed disappointed by his answer.

He took her hands in his and gazed down at her. In that moment he wished time could stand still, that he could find out all about her. Wished he could discover what happened between her and her father. Suddenly, it was imperative that he did. He wondered what had been so terrible that she had to run away from home. Wondered how she'd survived those years as a runaway.

"For what it's worth. I'm glad that I was the one nearby."

"Oh."

He bent down and gently kissed her forehead. "I'm going to leave now. You think you can manage? Do you need me to stay while you get ready for bed?"

She shook her head. "But, would you help me stand up before you go?"

He lifted her to a standing position.

"Ooo." She raised her hand to her forehead. "I feel woozy. What did you give me?"

"It'll wear off in a few hours. Then your ankle will hurt like the devil."

She held on to him while she tested her right foot. As soon as she put pressure on her injured ankle, she winced and gripped his side.

"I think I can manage. But, it's still plenty sore."

"It should be much better tomorrow."

As he started to release her, she swayed alongside him.

"Maybe you should lay back down." He helped her to her bed and once she was settled, he pulled the sheet over her body. "Get a good night's sleep. I'll check on you tomorrow."

# Chapter Twenty-Three

Annie woke up and stared at the low ceiling of the trailer. She moved her foot, slowly twisting it one way, then the other. It wasn't too bad today. Levi was right when he said it would feel better. Was the man always right? She slumped back on the bed and sighed. No need to rush this morning since she knew the lessons she'd be teaching the girls by heart.

She sat up and swung her legs off the bed. Placing her right foot on the floor, she gently tested it. After putting a small amount of pressure on it, she stood, careful to put most of her weight on her left foot. Between a combination of hopping and limping she made it to the bathroom. After her shower, and some ibuprofen, she made coffee.

With her pink chenille robe cinched around her waist, she tentatively stepped down the two front steps to the yard. The quiet mornings here at the RV Park were quite a change from the traffic noises in New York. She sipped on her coffee and allowed herself the luxury of silence.

After breakfast, she dressed in a sleeveless, pink and while floral dress, but when she tried to slip her injured foot in the strappy low-heeled sandal, she couldn't. It was way too tight, so she opted for a pair of sparkly flip-flops instead.

This morning was the first of her four Saturday sessions and she was really looking forward to it. Couldn't wait to meet the girls again. She enjoyed working with that age group, loved their excitement and how they lived in the moment.

She grabbed her large tote, then headed to her car. She walked slowly, careful not to put too much pressure on her injured side, and ended up limping to compensate. Just as she got to her car door, she spotted the sheriff's cruiser crunching up the drive toward her. She brushed a wayward strand of hair from her cheek and waited for him to stop.

* * *

"Good morning. I thought you might need a ride to-day," he said.

She was beautiful, standing there with her pink lips slightly parted in surprise. After last night, he thought of every excuse he could to come back here. Offering her a ride to the high school seemed a plausible solution. No use fighting his attraction to her. He was human after all.

She looked suspiciously at his squad car. "Your car or mine?" she said.

He grinned. "Have you ever ridden in a squad car?" He rapped on the hood. "This souped-up Dodge Charger is specially equipped with everything a law enforcement officer needs. Lots of bells and whistles. It's fun."

Her face suddenly clouded over and her formerly quizzical expression became serious, almost haunted. His ribs slammed into his chest. Oh, God. She had. And from her expression it must have been very unpleasant. He glanced at his car, then back at her and wondered if her look had anything to do with her cop father and the fact that she was a runaway.

"No, I haven't." She'd pulled herself together and the haunted expression faded.

She was lying. He'd swear on his life that she'd been in a squad car before and not under the best of circumstances.

"We can take yours if you want. I'm not on duty." He held out his hand to her.

She gazed at him not understanding. "Give me your key. You shouldn't be driving with that foot. If you have to slam on the brakes—"

"Oh, right. Of course." She shook her head like she was cleaning out cobwebs. After he helped her get in, she handed him her key. "Thanks for the lift."

"No problem. Happy to be of service."

The corners of her pink mouth quirked.

"I have to say this car is much better than that bug Liddy drives. Quite an improvement, actually."

He stuck his tongue in his cheek and kept his eye on the road in front of him. Annie seemed unusually quiet. There was so much he wanted to know about her. Especially, her past. What she loved? Hated? Her favorite food. Damn, he felt like he was back in high school on his first date with head cheerleader, Marsha Nolan.

"So. I know a little about your modeling career but what about your life before New York? Where are you from originally?" He glanced at her profile.

"No place in particular." Annie darted her eyes to her right and gazed out the window. "I moved around a lot."

He knew from his research, that that wasn't true. She'd only lived in two places according to her father's employment record. She squirmed in her seat.

"That must have been either a lot of fun for you or a nightmare."

"What do you mean?"

"Oh, you know. Having to change schools, having to make new friends. You know, starting over. I'm sure that was hard for you."

"Oh, yeah. It was." She turned her head away and gazed out the window. "Hey, there's one of your signs." She spread her hand through space. "Re-elect Sheriff Hawke."

He glanced at her. *Good try, Annie.* He wasn't about to let her change the subject. "So. Where was the last place you lived, before New York?"

Annie twisted her hands in her lap and her small, resigned sigh told him she'd have to answer or it would appear odd.

"What is this the third degree?" She laughed nervously.

He shrugged. "I'm just interested, that's all."

"Iowa. I lived in Iowa."

They pulled up at the school about forty-five minutes before the girls were to arrive. A smiling Amanda Marsh met them at the entrance.

"Do you need any help bringing anything in?" Amanda asked.

Annie shook her head as Levi lifted the large tote.

"It's all in here," he said.

"Great. Follow me."

They followed her down the wide hallway to one of the classrooms. It was a cheery well-lit room with long windows overlooking a small courtyard.

"This is a nice space," Annie said.

Amanda motioned to Levi to set the bag on one of the tables, then turned her attention to Annie. "It is isn't it? It was last year's Senior Class gift to the school. It's a study hall for seniors only. The lower classmen walk by and drool."

"I bet they do," Levi said. "My office doesn't have a view like this." He pulled out a chair for Annie. "I'm going for a coffee run. What do you ladies want?"

"There's coffee in the teacher's lounge," Amanda said.

"No thanks, Amanda. I actually prefer coffee to lighter fuel. I'm going to Café Con Leche. Any takers? Last chance."

"I'll take anything mocha, extra hot and large," Annie said.

"Nothing for me." Amanda chuckled. "I'll get mine from the lounge. I'm partial to turpentine."

* * *

Nine teenage girls, between the ages of fifteen and sixteen, showed up for Annie's talk. After giving each one a colorful notebook filled with the month's agenda, she had them sit in a large circle and introduce themselves.

They were a lively, chatty group and most of them were already good friends. And Annie knew before the month was over they will have bonded even more. She ended the session and gave each girl a lavender tote bag with the words, Like No Other, embossed in glittering, hot pink across the center.

After she gathered her belongings she turned toward the door and caught Levi watching her. He pushed away from the doorframe and entered the room. She wondered how long he'd been standing there.

"I'd ask how it went, but from the smiles on their faces, I'd say they had a great time."

She nodded and grinned. "We had a blast." She folded the extra lavender bags and placed them in her tote. "I've never worked with small town girls before."

"That sounds a bit condescending."

"Oh, I didn't mean it that way." She stepped around the desk. "Until recently, Like No Other has always been in larger cities, the inner cities, actually." She stopped and gazed up at him. "What I meant was, this was a special group of young women. I actually enjoyed their company and I'm going to really enjoy getting to know them." It was important he understand that she wasn't some New York City snob. That she got these girls. Understood them. She was a small town girl, too.

He smiled at her. A smile that lit his eyes and her bones melted. She was falling for him. Since she'd run away from home, she swore she'd never let a man rule her, much less care for what they thought of her. She'd had no use for men. Her father's treatment of her had seen to that. But Levi Hawke's very existence, his very presence challenged that belief. In that moment, she realized she'd been wrong to put every man in the same category as her father. Then the strangest thing happened. For the first time in her life she wondered what could have happened to her father to make him the way he was.

"Are you ready?" Levi asked.

"Yes." She jabbed a sheaf of papers in the top of her tote.

"Here. Let me get that." Levi secured the large tote bag over his shoulder. "So how did an Iowa girl end up in New York?"

*Back to twenty questions, I see.* "I went there to pursue a modeling career." She limped along beside him. "I was fortunate to meet Liz Connors, who, lord love her, saw something in me. Before I knew it, I was signed with her agency and getting booked for sessions. But, enough about me. Now tell—" She slipped on a scrap of paper in the hallway. Levi snaked his arm out and grabbed her around her waist, securing her to his side. She sucked in her breath and gazed up at him.

"You okay?"

She nodded and clung to him. She was in heaven. The warmth from his firm chest making her swoon. He released her and they continued down the hallway to the front entrance.

"What were you saying?" he asked.

"I was just asking about you, your life." She shook her head and smiled. "Tell me something about you."

They got to the front entrance and Levi held the door for her. "I went to Florida State on a football scholarship."

"Impressive. What position?"

"Quarterback."

"Nice. Then you graduated top of your class, and went on to the police academy. Right?"

"Exactly. Except for the top of the class part."

She chuckled. Underneath that entire macho act was a really nice guy.

* * *

"Would you like some lunch?" Levi asked.

She hesitated and seemed unsure of herself. Or, was it him? Maybe he needed to ease up on the questions. He could tell she was about to decline, but then she surprised him.

"Sure. I'd love some."

"There's a great little oyster bar on Market Street. The atmosphere is nice, too. It's right on the water."

She groaned.

"You don't like oysters?"

"Not really. I find them extremely nasty."

Annie's entire body shivered, which he found delightful. Her candid and sometimes physical reaction to things pleased him, which made watching her a pleasure. He could not deny his growing attraction and wondered if she felt it, too. He realized he may have misjudged her as every minute with her fueled his desire for more minutes, more hours, and more days. Today, he'd returned to the school early and had stood just outside the doorway watching her. The girls were practically hypnotized by Annie's contagious laughter and vivacious personality. In that moment, she'd even mesmerized him.

"You're in the oyster capital of the world."

"Sorry." She shuddered. "Not impressed."

Her expression looked like that of a child who'd just been given a spoonful of cod liver oil. He laughed. "Have you ever tasted them?"

"Yes. They're disgusting."

"Do you trust me?"

She cut her beautiful eyes in his direction. She seemed to be about to say something, but stopped and pressed her lips together.

"Well?" he asked when she didn't answer.

She glanced down at her hands. Her fingers were laced together all prim and proper like she was demonstrating one of her charm school examples. Then she turned her eyes on him and smiled. A lovely, sweet, heart-stopping smile.

"Yes. I trust you."

* * *

Ten minutes later they had ordered drinks and were sitting comfortably at a window in Cole's Oyster Bar, overlooking the gulf.

Cole set their drinks in front of them, a beer for Levi and iced tea for her. "What'll it be folks?"

"We'll have the steamed oysters," Levi said, not opening the menu.

"You got it." Cole took their menus and walked to a nearby table.

"This is such a cool part of town," Annie said.

"It's our historic district. Some of the shops have changed over the years, but the buildings and the wharf are just like they were in the early 1900s."

"Untouched and authentic. I like it." She gazed out across the water. A colorful variety of sailboats and fishing boats were stacked side by side along the docks.

"Imagine how they've changed in all these years." She nodded toward the docks.

"We still have a few ancient ones around, though most are in dry dock. Not used anymore."

"Why not?"

"It takes money to restore them. Just like most communities, we've experienced the economic slowdown."

"Here you go." Cole set two plates of steamed oysters, a basket of saltines, drawn butter, and horseradish in front of them. He slapped the bill on the corner of the table. "Let me know if you need anything else."

Annie looked aghast at the plate in front of her. "I really, *really* don't want this."

Levi laughed. It was deep and sexy and did all kinds of tingly things to her heart. "Okay, Sheriff, show me how to eat this stuff."

"Okay. This is how a newbie eats oysters. First, you make your own cocktail sauce. Mix catsup and horseradish in this little cup."

She watched him stir the two ingredients into the small container.

"You too. Go on, mix your own."

She poured the catsup in the cup provided, then dunked her fork into the horseradish.

"Not too much or your ears will steam and your nose will scream."

"Okay." She laughed.

"Next, you take a saltine. Like so," he continued with the lesson, holding up the small white square cracker in his fingers.

She followed his lead.

"Now, dip the oyster in the butter, then place it on the center of the cracker." He waited as she followed his directions. "Now, top it off with the horseradish sauce."

"Gross."

"No complaining. You're almost there. No. Don't bite into it," he said, as she was about to do just that. "Pop the entire thing in your mouth." Which he proceeded to do with gusto. "Mmm. Trust me, you won't be disappointed."

She closed her eyes.

"What are you doing?"

"I'm hoping that if I don't have to see it, it won't taste too bad."

"Come on. On the count of three. One. Two. Three."

Prepared for the worst dining experience of her life, Annie opened her mouth and shoved the entire cracker inside, then brought the napkin to her lips, fully prepared to spit it out.

She glanced at Levi, who waited with an expectant light in his eyes. She didn't say anything, just swallowed and immediately fixed herself another cracker. She popped that one in her mouth. This time with her eyes open. "You know, this is pretty darn good."

He grinned. A boyish, I told you so grin.

"Okay, you were right." She fixed herself another. "But, I still don't think I could ever eat one raw."

"Trust me. You'll get there."

*Trust me.* Was this some sort of a test? She heard those words many times from the opposite sex and she'd never believed them. Not after life with her father. For the past ten years she'd stashed her emotions regarding men on a high, out-of-the-way shelf. Occasionally, she'd take them down and dust them off, only to set them back up after the inevitable disappointment.

She glanced at the steamed mollusks staring up at her. It would be nice to trust someone again, even if only about oysters. She raised her eyes to his. They held a delicious gleam she found devastatingly appealing. Maybe, it wouldn't hurt to start trusting again, just a little bit.

* * *

Levi watched a myriad of emotions cross her pretty face. She was lost in thought and he wished like the devil she'd confide in him. He knew from past experience women didn't usually open up to him. And with his reputation as the 'bully sheriff', he wasn't at all surprised. But, he wanted that image to change, especially where she was concerned. If anyone had told him a month ago that he would be sitting in Cole's Oyster Bar flirting and teasing with a beautiful brunette, he'd have arrested them for slander.

Annie stirred a packet of sugar in her tea, squeezed several lemon wedges into her drink, and stirred some more.

"Okay, spill," she said.

He blinked. "What do you mean?" Levi sat back in his chair and gave her an innocent look.

She leaned forward and placed her forearms on the table. "You've been unusually nice to me these past few days and I'd like to know why."

He paused, tempering what he was about to say. "I'd like to get to know you. Is that so hard to understand? You're a beautiful, intelligent woman. A man would be crazy not to want to get to know you."

"Vey prettily said, Sheriff. But, I'm still not buying it. You don't like me. Haven't from the first moment. I know what you think of me." She sighed and leaned back in her seat. "This is about Alex, isn't it?"

"Actually, it's not. But, I'm all ears, if there's anything you'd like to tell me about him."

"I knew it."

"You know nothing of the sort." He reached across the Formica tabletop and took hold of her hand. "You brought up Alex Langdon. I didn't. Would I like to know about your relationship with him? Yes. But it's because I want to know everything about *you*. You're right about one thing. I didn't like Anna Delany too much, but I like Annie Dell. And I'd like to get to know *both* of you." He smiled at her, hoping she'd trust him if only a little.

He understood Annie more that she realized. After the death of his sister he'd erected a wall of his own not unlike Annie's. Except his was self-imposed, driven by his own guilt. Whereas Annie's more than likely stemmed from her father's abuse. He'd turned inward, shutting down his emotions to the world around him. Knew he was doing it and frankly, didn't care. But the young Annie had had no choice.

But he was human, all right. Filled with emotions, and longings just like everyone else in the world. Annie had literally sped past him and brought it to the fore. She'd rolled into town, challenged and tormented him like those damn, black, biting "dog flies" brought in by the June Grass and the North winds. No amount of swatting could drive them away or stop their invariable sting.

And buddy, did she sting. Smack dab in the center of his heart. She made him bleed reminding him he *was* human, after all.

He watched the tension leave her body and she visibly relaxed, letting out a lovely sigh.

"Do you mean it? You're not…" She shook her head. "Just saying this?"

She looked suddenly vulnerable. How did she do that? Go from a no-nonsense, savvy woman to a child, needing assurance. He nodded, slowly, deliberately, keeping his eyes on her the entire time. "Remember when I asked you if you'd trust me?"

She pursed her lips and a tiny spark of worry filled her radiant eyes.

He gathered her other hand and held them both. "I wasn't only referring to oysters."

Her honey brown eyes twinkled, chasing away the worry that lingered there only seconds ago. Pink lips turned up at the corners revealing a tiny dimple he hadn't noticed before. How had he missed that? It gave her that girl next-door appeal. No wonder she was so good at her job. The many faces of Annie. Sexy, beguiling, innocent, and now the girl next door. God help him, he wanted to know them all.

# Chapter Twenty-Four

"What does the word poise, mean? Anyone?" Annie glanced around the classroom at the upturned animated faces.

"Grace," Susan said.

"Good. Give me another."

Tonya raised hand and Annie acknowledged her. "Elegance."

"Love that word." Annie glanced around the room. "Anyone else?" She noticed Beth's eyes were downcast. "Beth, can you think of a word?"

Beth glanced up, wide-eyed and stared at Annie. "Um, balance?"

"Yes. Balance. Very good. And, I can't think of a better word to take us into the next segment."

Annie reached behind her and grabbed a large textbook from the desk, balanced it on her head, then walked gracefully from one side of the room to the other. "Michele, you've been awfully quiet, so I think I'll start with you."

The girls laughed in unison as Michele stepped up to the front of the room.

"Okay Michele, let's show this snickering group just what you're made of. Stand up straight." Annie centered the textbook on top of Michele's head, then slowly released it.

Michele stiffened and stood perfectly still.

"Now walk," Annie said.

Michele took a step forward. The book teetered, Michele squealed, and the book fell to the floor. Laughter flooded the room.

"You're next, Tonya, let's see what you've got."

Tonya jumped up and hurried to the front. The book lasted two seconds longer on her head then it did on Michele's. For the next thirty minutes, each girl took their turn, then another until every one of them could walk with the book balanced on their head.

Beth was the last one to accomplish this task successfully, and when she did, cheers went up around the room.

"Hey. Hey. What's all this noise?" Levi poked his head in the doorway.

Ten heads swiveled in his direction. He was wearing a cobalt blue v-neck t-shirt and jeans and he looked fantastic.

"Am I going to have to arrest you guys?"

Laughter floated across the room. Annie flipped the book in her hands and gazed out at the sweet sea of smiling faces. "Are you guys thinking what I'm thinking?"

"Yes," they yelled.

"You're next, Sheriff."

Sheriff Hawke was happy to oblige. And when he placed the book on top of his head the teens giggled, then cheered him on. He took one step and the book tumbled off his head. Both Annie and Levi dove to catch the book. Together, they caught it just before it hit the ground.

"Good catch, Miss Annie," he said.

"You too, Sheriff," she said, locking eyes with his.

"See you at lunch?" he whispered.

"I'll be there."

Levi winked at the girls and waved good-bye. Annie was amazed at how warm and attentive he was with them. He'd laughed and joked like an older brother. Yes, he definitely had a way with the women. Including her. He was attentive, charming, and adorable. And it was clear he enjoyed the girls' company. And from the glowing faces gazing at his departing back, it looked like the feeling was mutual.

* * *

Levi watched Annie push through the screened door at Cole's Oyster Bar and lifted his arm to get her attention. When she got to the table, she slung her purse on the bench seat and slid in across from him.

"It must be nice to be the boss and schedule every Saturday off," she quipped.

"We alternate months between us. I scheduled this month around Like No Other. Since I'm the local chairman and all."

"Speaking of that." She placed both forearms on the table and leaned toward him. "You were great with the girls today."

God she was beautiful. All bubbly and excited about life.

"I didn't know you were going to stop by," she said.

He shrugged. "Just doing my job." *And taking every opportunity to be near you.*

"What did you order for me today?" she asked.

He couldn't help but smile at her enthusiasm. "I have to hand it to you, for a high fashion model, you sure do like to eat."

"I know. And if I'm not careful," she playfully slapped her thigh, "it'll catch up with me, too. So. What did you order for me?"

"Patience, sweetheart. You'll see."

Annie beamed at him, then reached across the table and gently took his hand. "Are we dating?"

He cocked his head to the side. "What do you think?"

"I think we're dating." She released his hand and sat back while Cole poured their iced tea.

"Hello, Miss Annie." Cole set a small plate of lemon wedges on the table.

"Oh, you remembered. Thank you." She plucked a yellow wedge from the plate and squeezed lemon juice into her tea. Then another and another, until she'd squeezed three lemon wedges dry.

"They do have lemonade here, you know."

"I'm not making lemonade. I just like a lot of lemon in my tea." Annie wiped her lemony fingers on her napkin. When she finished, she lifted her eyes to him. "Where were we?"

She smiled, revealing that single dimple on the side of her mouth. A mouth he wanted to kiss, and kiss, and kiss.

At that moment Cole appeared with their fried oyster, New Orleans style, po-boy sandwiches and seafood gumbo. Rich spices emanated from the savory Cajun dish.

"What do you think?" Levi asked.

"Wow. This looks wonderful."

Before Cole set the rest of the food on the table Annie dipped her spoon into the gumbo, then raised the spicy liquid to her parted lips. Her eyes closed and she moaned.

"Cole, this is divine."

Levi glanced from Annie to Cole and grinned. Cole beamed, delighted in Annie's enjoyment of the dish.

"Why thank you, Miss Annie."

"Cole's from New Orleans. He came here after hurricane Katrina," Levi said.

"Oh, I didn't know. Well, this is fabulous."

"Thank you. Let me know if you need anything else."

Cole strode away pleased with his new conquest.

Levi unwrapped his po-boy. "You've made his day."

"It wasn't hard. This is fabulous."

"Okay, now for oyster fest number two," Levi said. "Go ahead. Try the sandwich. The bread is baked in New Orleans and flown in every morning. It's not like any other French bread you've ever had."

She bit into the crispy fried oyster sandwich and her eyes widened in delight. Breadcrumbs went everywhere.

She swallowed and took a swig of her tea. "That. Is. Incredible. The crust is like a pastry. But what a mess."

"It flakes all over the place. The reason for that." He nodded toward the white paper the sandwich was served in. "Easy clean up."

"So I see."

After the meal, Cole served them each a slice of key lime pie and hot coffee. "Oh, no. I can't eat another bite."

"Would you like for me to box it up for you?" Cole asked.

"Let me take a bite first." She cut into the firm confection, then slid the fork between her lips. "Heavenly." She took another bite and then another.

Levi glanced at Cole. "I don't think we'll need that to-go box."

Cole nodded and grinned.

* * *

Annie slid the key into the white, aluminum door of the trailer and pushed it open. Levi stepped in behind her and entwined his arms around her waist. "Come here, you." He pulled her to his chest and feathered kisses along her neck, then spun her around to face him. She rose to her toes and lifted her face to his. Her warm, parted lips trembled with desire.

He'd been mesmerized by those lips all through lunch and had thought of little else but claiming them for his own. No time like the present. His lips met hers. She tasted of sweet limes and cream bringing to mind another kind of dessert.

He lifted her in his arms and carried her to the small sofa. His lips trailed along her cheek before re-claiming her mouth.

They crashed onto the seat cushions and when he paused to maneuver her to the side, they both slipped off and hit the floor.

"Ouch," Annie half laughed and cried. "What are you trying to do?"

He stopped and held her against his chest. He was flat on his back and she was sprawled on top of him. "You know, I think there's actually more room down here."

She giggled, burrowed closer and slid her arms around his neck. She turned her head sideways and snuggled alongside him.

"I can hear your heart beat. My, that's fast." She raised her head and grinned. "I can't imagine why?"

"Come back down here and I'll show you why."

She happily complied.

"You're as light as a feather. Which is beyond under-standing with the way you eat." Even though she was tall, firm, and extremely well put together, she didn't weigh a thing.

Annie pulled a small pillow from the couch. He braced himself for the smack he figured was coming, but instead, she tucked it underneath his head.

"Comfy?" she asked.

"Hum-Mmm."

Tenderly, almost reverently, she placed her mouth over his. He moaned, loving her gentle touch. She was scrumptious, tantalizing, and driving him crazy. She lifted her head, laced her hands together across his chest, and gazed at him.

"That's it? That's all I get?" he said.

She twinkled down at him.

"Would you like to hear a confession, Officer?"

God, she was adorable. "Uh, oh."

Annie giggled. "Is that a yes?"

"Spill, woman."

She licked her lips, sending all kinds of delightful shivers down his spine. Her lovely face was very close to his and he was amazed at her complexion. She was cover girl radiant. Beautiful, and not only on the outside. She sparkled down at him.

Spending the past couple of weeks with her had been an eye opening experience. She'd revealed a side of herself that she'd kept well hidden in the early days he'd been around her. Delightful, feminine and intelligent. She was all of that and more, and he was falling for her.

"I've never had a boyfriend before," she said unexpectedly, then ran her fingers along his right temple. "Does that surprise you?"

It certainly did. "What about Alex Lang—"

She placed a slender finger over his lips and shook her head. "Please. Don't ruin this moment. Don't even mention his name. He was never my boyfriend."

"Okay." The entire country believed she and Alex had been an item. And until this moment, he sure as heck thought so, too. Fine, he'd save that conversation for another day. "Surely you've had boyfriends, though. You're beautiful. Intelligent." He grinned. "A termagant."

"Hey, watch it buster. I have you at my mercy right now. Don't think I won't use it."

He laughed. "I'd like to see you try."

That got an audacious grin from her. She lowered her head, her mouth hovered over his and whispered. "Since I've never had a boyfriend. The only thing I know is what I've seen in movies. Read in books. I bet you could teach me a few things. Give me some *real* experience."

She kissed him then. With slow. Deliberate. Pecks. Tiny fishhooks, reeling him in with each sweet, peck of her lips.

He groaned. "You're killing me, woman."

"That's the idea, Sheriff. Softly. Like the song says."

"To hell with softly." His arms banded tightly around her. "Let the lessons begin."

He crushed her to him, teaching her then and there what a real kiss was all about. In all of its passion and sexy aggression. He rolled over, taking her with him until she was underneath him. He arched his body sideways to keep his full weight off her. She gazed at him, her eyes dark with desire, and her small hands crept around his neck. He kissed her again and felt the earth move beneath him. He ran his hand along her ribcage, settling his palm on her waist. His kiss deepened. Urgency and strength drove him. He moaned and lifted his head. "Oh, sweet, sweetheart. I need to stop or I may not." He ran his fingers over her temple and brushed her hair from her face. Desire flowed from her beautiful, glowing eyes. It would be so easy to keep going.

He fell against her and groaned. She laughed and he raised his head. "Oh sure. I can see you don't know what you're doing."

"I don't, really." She gazed up at him all innocent-eyed. "You're just a great teacher."

"Right." He kissed her nose, then stood to his feet and looked down at her.

Annie sat up and drew her knees to her chest. Hair tousled and dreamy-eyed, she sat on the floor looking up at him with a goofy smile on her face. A rosy hue covered her cheeks and it warmed his heart just looking at her.

He smiled and offered her a hand up. In one swift motion his arms circled her waist, bringing her close. "I'll see you later, gator."

She chuckled. "I never pegged you for silly."

He hugged her to him. "You bring out the man I used to be, before…"

She tilted her head and gazed up at him. "Before what?"

"Nothing." He kissed her. "That one's for the road." He winked, then left.

# Chapter Twenty-Five

Annie leaned on the doorframe and waved goodbye, wondering what *nothing* he was talking about. Mark had told Liddy there was something from Levi's past that'd bothered him. Annie huffed out air from between her lips, picked up the pillow, then plopped down and hugged it to her chest.

She'd taken a chance telling him she'd never had a boyfriend. She'd forgotten about Alex until Levi said his name. She'd have to explain Alex to him sometime, not that there was much there. Certainly, a relationship, but not the kind the world assumed. It consisted of separate bedrooms, separate lives, and the occasional gala event for appearances' sake.

Annie decided to take a walk in the woods, but this time she'd take her phone and stay near the perimeter. Besides, there was plenty of daylight left.

After changing into jeans, a white cotton sleeveless blouse, and sneakers, she tucked her phone in her back pocket and left.

A light breeze feathered her face and released the ever-present pine scent. Inhaling deeply she gave way to the memories of her last walk in these woods. She shook her head, pushing them aside. This afternoon would be different.

She entered the woods and this time kept the RV Park firmly in her sights. She meandered through the pines careful to keep the park on her left.

The quiet soothed and comforted her like a warm blanket on a chilly night. Pine infused her senses. She would miss this after she was gone.

The forest grounds were dotted with a variety of wild flowers, which she hadn't noticed the other day. She bent to inspect a yellow one with an orange center. Lovely. So tiny yet so perfect. This would be a great example to use with the girls. They, too, were beautifully formed, one of a kind creations, but so many of them felt far from unique or beautiful.

A sharp cry penetrated the quiet. Heart thudding, she shot upright. Someone was crying. She stood perfectly still and waited. It came from up ahead. To get her bearings, she glanced to her left. No way was she getting lost today. She could still see the park through the trees.

Gnawing her bottom lip, she crept forward. She didn't want to surprise whoever it was or embarrass herself in the process. She paused. Maybe she should leave well enough alone. What business was it of hers anyway? This person was definitely female and Annie wasn't worried about getting hurt or anything, but still. She remembered her own secret bouts of tears as a girl. Terrified to tell anyone what was going on with her policeman father - the town's shining example of all that was right and good in Rockford. Pillar of the community and all that, jazz. Whenever she'd come close to telling someone, she'd balk. What if they didn't believe her, then she'd have to go home and face his anger. That she could never risk.

She crept along, cringing at the crunch of pine needles, which until this moment hadn't seemed loud at all.

She peeked around one of the larger trees. A teenage girl sat on the ground with her head against her knees.

Annie ducked back behind the tree, suddenly very sad. It was Beth Sanders. The shy girl in her Saturday group. She had no idea Beth lived here. Annie closed her eyes, breathed a quick prayer for wisdom, then stepped out into the open.

"Beth honey. Are you okay?" *Of course she wasn't okay. What a stupid question.*

Beth's head shot up and she scrambled to her feet. She quickly swiped her face.

"Annie." Beth's eyes widened. "I, um. Yeah, I'm okay. It's nothing."

Sure it was, nothing. That red palm mark on her arm was probably nothing. Just like the time Liddy had noticed a similar red mark on Annie's wrist. That was nothing, too.

"Do you want to talk about it?"

Beth shook her head.

Annie placed her hand on Beth's shoulder. "Well if you ever want to talk to me, I want you to know that whatever you say will stay between us."

Beth nodded and stared at the ground.

"Would you like to walk with me? It's a beautiful afternoon," Annie said.

"No. I should get back. My dad is probably looking for me. I don't want to get into any trouble."

"Trouble? What kind of trouble?"

"I said it was nothing." Then, like a gazelle, Beth bounded through the forest.

Annie watched Beth run through the trees, hair flowing behind her. She was a beautiful girl with her long dark hair and high cheekbones. Model material. Annie had always wanted to open her own modeling agency. Maybe Beth could be her first client.

Losing interest in her walk, Annie went back to the trailer park. When she entered the clearing she glanced around the area. She'd met most of her immediate neighbors but not everyone. She wandered through the compound, reading the names on the mailboxes but didn't see Sanders.

She walked across the park to Pete's trailer and knocked.

Seconds later, he pushed the squeaky door open. "Afternoon, Annie. Would you like to come in?"

"No thanks. I'm just looking for a family. I heard one of the girls in my Saturday morning group lives here. The name is Sanders. Can you tell me her trailer number?"

"Humm," He scratched his head. "We don't have a Sanders."

"The girl's first name is Beth."

"Oh, Beth. Sure. She lives with her stepfather. Dave Franklin. They're in camp six."

"Great. Thanks."

"You take any more evening walks?"

"I just got back from one."

"Good to see you made it this time." He chuckled and ducked back in his Airstream.

Annie walked with purpose toward her cute little home, but veered left to approach the doublewide trailer and knocked. She heard the crash of what sounded like glass coming from inside. A muffled curse, then seconds later the door swung open.

A disheveled man sporting an intense frown stood before her. He was holding a dishcloth and there was blood on one of his hands. His shirt was soaking wet and he reeked of alcohol. A pair of bloodshot eyes stared down at her.

At the sight of the blood, Annie's heart went into over-time. She swallowed hard and stared at him.

"May I help you?"

He barked the words and it was obvious to her she'd interrupted something. She craned her neck trying to see inside the room behind him. "Hi, I'm sorry to bother you…but are you okay?" She nodded toward his hand. He continued to wipe the blood as she spoke.

"It's nothing." He wrapped the cloth around his wound. "And who are you?"

"I'm sorry, I'm in Number 7, the little pink and white trailer. I just wanted to introduce myself. I'm Annie Dell and your daughter, Beth, is participating in my Saturday group, Like No Other."

He nodded briskly. "Yes, she's really enjoying it. But, as you can see, you've caught me at a bad time. I'd really like to visit with you, but now is not the time. I'm sorry."

Before she could reply, he shut the door in her face.

* * *

"Dave Franklin? Are you sure?"

"Yes, yes I'm sure. He had blood on his hand and reeked of cheap wine. And having just found Beth in the woods crying her eyes out, I felt I needed to report him."

"Okay. I'll talk to him."

"No! You can't just confront him...I mean, can you?"

"Annie. I know what I'm doing. You need to stay out of it. I've known Dave and Beth for years. His wife recently died and this has been a difficult time for them both."

That bit of news only fueled Annie's thoughts. Her dad had become a monster after her mom died.

"I'm sure you're mistaken about him," Levi broke into her musings. "But I'll check it out. My way. All right?"

"All right."

* * *

The next morning, Levi drove over to Pete's RV Park, pulled up in front of Dave's home, and got out. He thought about how best to approach Dave and decided to just come out with it.

Dave opened the door, an expression of pleasant surprise on his face. "Levi. Come in. I was just making coffee. Will you join me?"

"I'd love a cup."

Dave poured them both a cup and motioned for Levi to take a seat. Dave smiled tentatively at him. "So, what's going on? It's not Beth, is it? She's having a tough time since her mom died."

"That's what I'm here to find out." He glanced at Dave's bandaged hand. "Are you guys doing okay? Any problems?"

"That sounds ominous. What's going on, Levi?"

Levi set the mug on the side table and leaned toward Dave. "We got a call from a concerned citizen. It seems Beth has some marks on her arms that look suspicious." He held his breath. Waiting.

Dave's jaw clenched. "Let me guess. Was the citizen your little friend?"

Levi clasped his hands together. "Yes. She came across Beth crying in the woods yesterday and noticed red marks on her arms."

"And she came to my door investigating." He shook his head, set his cup on the table, and stood to his feet. "For God's sake, Levi. You know me!"

"That's why I'm here instead of Social Services."

"So you think I'm, what? Daddy Dearest? Good Lord. I would never nor have I ever laid a hand on Beth. Step-daughter, yes. But I love her like my own."

"Annie says she came to your door yesterday and that you had all the signs of someone who'd been drinking. That your hands were covered in blood. She said before you opened the door, she heard a crash, like glass breaking. So she was concerned."

Levi stayed seated and looked up at him. He didn't want Dave to feel threatened. He knew Dave and hoped like hell there was a good explanation to all this.

Dave strode across the room and wrenched open a small panty door. There must have been over a hundred brown bottles lined up in neat rows on the shelves.

Levi stood and walked over to the cabinet. "Is that beer?"

"Yes. I've started making beer. Yesterday I was steriliz-ing a couple of glass carboys and I accidently broke one on the sink." Dave lifted his hand to Levi's face. "I had to have twelve stitches. Hence, the blood."

Dave was clearly exasperated and Levi couldn't blame him.

"In the process, I knocked over ten bottles I'd already filled. Beer and glass shattered everywhere. All over me and the floor."

Dave folded his arms across his chest. "And as for the bloodshot eyes. I haven't slept much since Deb died." He blew air from between his lips. "I hope that clears up any of your doubts?"

Levi's stomach churned. "Dave I'm so sorry," he said. "But I had to check."

Dave was livid as he saw Levi to the door and Levi couldn't blame him. If something like that got around in a small town like theirs, it could ruin a man, even if it wasn't true.

"Levi?"

Levi paused at the door and looked back at Dave.

"Look. I'm mad as hell at Annie Dell, but something has been bothering Beth." Dave pressed his fingers to his forehead. "If Beth was in the woods crying, then it must be worse than I thought." He shoved his hands in his pockets. "I guess I should be thanking my nosy neighbor. If someone's hurting Beth, I'll find out."

"Don't do anything stupid."

"I won't."

Levi closed the door behind him and walked back to Annie's.

She burst out of her trailer just as he approached, skidding to a stop in front of him "Well? What happened? What'd he say?"

"Annie. You almost ruined a man's life. Thank God you didn't call Social Services."

Her honey brown eyes widened in horror.

"You didn't. Tell me you didn't."

"I did. She's— Oh, no. Is that her?"

Levi turned at the sound of the approaching car. He swore. "It is."

"Why is she coming here?"

"I don't know," Levi said. "Let's hope she hasn't called him yet."

"Brenda." Levi waved her over. "We need to talk to you."

Brenda Cunningham climbed out of her car and shook Levi's hand. "And I need to talk to her. Are you Annie?"

Annie shot a worried glance at Levi, focused on Brenda, and continued. "Yes, and I am so sorry. Apparently, I've made a terrible mistake." She glanced back at Levi for support.

"She's right," Levi said. "I've just talked with Dave and found out why Annie assumed the worst." He glanced over at Annie, then back at Brenda. "Please tell me you haven't called him yet."

"I haven't. I wanted to talk with Annie first." She gave Annie her full attention. "What happened to make you accuse Dave of this?"

Levi listened to Annie explain what she'd witnessed, first with Beth and then with Dave.

"Since it was only about twenty minutes from the time I saw Beth to when I met Dave, I assumed the worst."

Contrition lit Annie's beautiful eyes. Pleading for him to understand. And he did. He knew where she was coming from but that didn't make it acceptable to go around calling the police and social services on a hunch.

"Do you realize what you could have heaped on this good man?" Brenda said.

"Yes. I'll go over there right now and apologize. But you need to leave before he sees you. Please."

Brenda, nodded, shook Levi's hand, then got back in her car and left.

Annie turned remorseful eyes in his direction. "Will you come with me?"

"Yeah. Let's get it over with. But, I need to warn you, he's mad as hell. Get prepared to get chewed up and spit out."

Annie and Levi stood quietly in front of Dave Franklin's door and waited. Except for the wringing of her hands, one would never know she was nervous. With chin raised and body erect she silently waited for whatever she had coming. Dave thought she was some meddling busybody. But Levi understood what'd motivated her actions and suddenly realized he was the *only* one who did. The thought humbled him.

Dave opened the door. His jaw clenched when he recognized Annie.

"Mr. Franklin. Please accept my apology. I'm so, so sorry. I completely misunderstood what I saw yesterday. I was just worried about Beth—"

"Please." Dave raised his hand. "No more. I appreciate your concern for my daughter." He stopped abruptly. He was clearly angry.

"Please, let me finish." Annie spread her hands in appeal. "Beth said something about you being angry if she didn't get back home. And when she ran away from me, I assumed the worst. I meant well. I know I didn't handle this properly. Please forgive me."

He sighed heavily and stuffed his hands in his pockets, then turned his attention to Levi. "Since you left Beth has come home. I confronted her about the marks on her arm and found out she's been dating a boy I'd told her not to go out with. Apparently, she's been going out behind my back." He sighed. "Look, I need to get back to her. Thank you for your apology, Miss Dell."

He nodded to them both, then shut the door.

With head lowered, Annie turned slowly toward Levi. He walked her back to her place and followed her inside.

She plopped down on her couch and he could tell she was near tears. He sat down beside her and pulled her against him.

She put her face in her hands and stayed perfectly still. His heart ached for her.

"I'm so ashamed." Her entire body shuddered. "I hurt that man. I could see it in his eyes."

He turned her around so he could face her. She hung her head and wouldn't look at him.

"I'm so stupid." She stared at the floor.

Levi tilted her chin. "Look at me, honey."

She raised red eyes to his. "Don't you see? I did to him what I've accused others of doing to me. Not getting the facts. Jumping to conclusions." She shook her head. "And I've done the same thing to you. Assuming, because you wear a uniform and a badge, you're like—"

"Like who? Your father?"

She tensed and raised wide, questioning eyes to his face. "How do you know about him?"

"I have a confession to make. After the hurricane, I researched you."

Her trembling lips fell open. Her formerly distraught eyes now filled with anxiety.

"What?"

"I care about you a lot, Annie."

"You spied on me?" She shrugged away from him.

"Did you hear what I just said?" He took her hands and gently shook them. "I care about you."

She pulled her hands from his and stood. "My father used to spy on me."

"I didn't spy on you, dammit." He stood up. She shrank from him and took a step back. "What? You think I'm going to hurt you? You've spent weeks with me and that's what you think?"

"Don't make this about you," she said. "I thought I could trust you."

"You're being unreasonable."

"Please leave."

The anger and hurt in her eyes crushed him. "Fine. If that's what you want." He burst from her trailer like a bull from its pen. "Unreasonable. Pig headed. Female." He strode to his car and stopped. No. She was not getting off that easy. He turned on his heel and marched back to her trailer.

When he pushed open the door, Annie was standing, head lowered, at the small kitchen sink. Her head snapped up as he stepped into the trailer.

"I don't know what the hell he did to you, but I am *not* him. I'm sorry if I hurt you. I was looking into your connection with Alex. One link led to another. That's how I found out. That is my job and I make no excuses for doing it."

With her lovely face still etched in anxiety, she pressed her hand to her chest as if she was trying to calm her racing heart.

"I'm here for you, Annie. I care about you." He took one step toward her. "I think it's time you tell me your story. Please."

Her eyes softened and filled with resignation. "I care about you, too," she whispered, then stepped into his arms.

His heart soared at her confession and he pressed her close and held her until she was ready to talk.

# Chapter Twenty-Six

They settled onto the sofa where he took her back in his arms. "I like you here, Miss Annie Dell. Thanks for giving me another chance."

She gave him a half smile. "So. How much do you know?"

"That you ran away at age fifteen. That your father was a Rockford, Iowa cop. That he was fired from his previous post in Des Moines for drinking on the job." He continued to stroke her hair. "Why are you terrified of storms?" She started to cry and he held her tightly. Rage bubbled up inside of him. God, he wanted to hurt this man. He put Annie from him but kept a hold of her arms. "Talk to me. Whatever happened, I promise you, we'll face it together." He pulled her back to his chest and waited. "I'm not letting you go until you tell me every-thing."

"You have no idea what it's like for me to hear you say that."

"What do you mean, honey?"

"I was always on the outside wondering what it was like to have a father that loved me. Protected me."

"I know. Fathers are supposed to love and protect their little girls."

"Not hurt them," she said.

Her words, spoken so matter-of-factly, cut him like a knife.

"It was years after my mother died that I realized she'd tempered him while she was alive. But when her protection was gone, he was different. After her death, he drank more and more." She turned in his arms. "Hold me."

"I am holding you."

"No, like this." She lay back on his lap and he cradled her in his arms.

"I want to see your face." She placed her palm against his cheek. "You give me courage."

She smiled wistfully up at him and he wondered how he ever lived this life without her.

"My mother was beautiful," she said. "When he met her, she was a dancer. Nightclubs mainly. When my dad drank he'd accuse her of being unfaithful, terrible things like that. After she died, and my interest in being a model became evident to him, he told me I was just like her. And *that*, he wouldn't have."

She sat up, grabbed a tissue, and blew her nose, then lay back in his arms.

"There was this one time. I'd worked babysitting half the summer. I saved enough for a blouse I'd seen at Lulu's Dress Shop. It was pale yellow and had tiny rosebuds on it." She briefly closed her eyes. "It was beautiful. The first thing I ever bought with my own money. I was so excited. I came home from the store wearing it. He took one look and told me to take it off. He said it made me look like a slut."

Levi simmered with rage as he listened to Annie, but he kept himself under complete control, just like he was taught. He ran his fingers through her hair, brushing it off her forehead. "What happened?"

"He made me take it off. Afterwards, he took the kitchen knife and ripped it to pieces." A single tear fell from the corner of her eye onto his lap. "Then, he did what he always did to discipline me."

*Oh God, please help me to bear it.*

"We had this shed out back, near the creek. When I disobeyed him or even when he just thought I did, he'd take me out there and handcuff me to this pipe. It was like a towel bar or something, but bigger. Anyway, he'd cuff me to it and turn out the light, putting me in the dark. He'd shut the door and leave me."

*Sweet Jesus.*

"He never touched me, never hit me, and never even spanked me. He just chained me up like an animal."

"He was the animal." Disgust for this imitation of a father made him sick to his stomach.

Annie placed her hand against the side of his face. He grabbed it and held it there. "There's more," she said. "And then I'll be done."

He nodded and gazed down at her.

She gave him a watery smile. "I'm almost finished."

She took her hand from his face and looked away from him as if she couldn't bear to see the hurt and anger in his eyes. He could shoot himself for letting his emotions get the best of him. She needed him to be strong.

"The shed sat near our creek. It was June and we'd had a lot of rain. The creek was near overflowing."

"Dear God."

She smiled a sweet smile of understanding at him. "Not long after he cuffed me to the pipe, it started to pour. I waited, but he didn't come."

Her voice broke and he wrapped his arms around her, hugging her to him as much for his own comfort as hers.

"Levi, I'm all right. It's tough to tell the story, but you need to know I'm all right."

"Okay." He nodded. "Keep going."

"So, thirty minutes passed, then an hour, and still he didn't come."

He clenched his jaw and gazed at her face. He watched her lips move and her eyes cloud over. He glanced up and stared straight ahead. He wanted to kill this man.

Annie gripped his jaw with her fingers and forced him to look at her.

"It has a happy ending," she said.

"What do you mean?"

"Running away, hiding here from the media. It all led me to you."

Her serious face framed glowing eyes and a sweet smile. He lowered his head and gave her pink lips a soft kiss. He thought about the many times she'd shed tears since he'd known her. If there was anything worth crying about, this would be it. But she spoke with a calmness and clarity that garnered his respect and made him want to protect her even more.

He tenderly stroked her arm, then took her hand in his. "I think I know what's coming, next." His voice was low and sounded strange to his own ears.

She nodded. "The water rose, covering my shoes, and my ankles. I yanked at the handcuffs until my wrist bled. When the water level reached my knees, I knew I was going to die. Then, he burst through the door. I can still see the terror in his eyes. He un-cuffed me and carried me in the house. He was beside himself. Apparently, he'd fallen asleep in a drunken stupor.

"He begged me for forgiveness. Just like he always did after one of his punishments. After he was sober. Until one day, when I was fifteen, he shoved me against the wall for the last time. I'd run away before and he would always find me and bring me home in the back of his squad car. But this time, I knew it had to be for good."

He held her tightly against him. "It explains a lot," he said. "Why you felt the need to protect Beth. Your fear of storms. Why you fell apart when I cuffed you to the table."

She sat up, took Levi's face in her hands, and kissed him. He pushed a strand of her dark hair behind her ear and gazed into her eyes.

"I am so, so sorry," he said.

"I feel better having told you. I'm glad you insisted. And, I'm glad you came back." Her lips trembled a smile. "It's important you know I'm all right. You do, right?"

"I know you are." His arms tightened around her.

"I've been thinking about trying to find him," she said.

"You have?"

She nodded. "I feel like I need to see him."

He stiffened. "I don't think that's a good idea."

"Why?"

"My guess is he wouldn't want to see you."

"How can you be so sure?"

"Because he's had years to find you. He's a cop. Trust me, he knows how."

"Look. There are some things I'd like to say to him. Things I *need* to say to him. Then I'll be free."

"Do you even know where he is?"

"No. But I suspect you do." She arched a delicate brow and laid a look on him that reminded him of his former captain.

He clenched his jaw. "He's in a rehab program in Des Moines."

Her serious eyes searched his face. "You know I'm right."

"Actually, I don't know. But if that's what you want. I'll go with you. I won't have you seeing that monster by yourself."

* * *

Saturday morning the girls came in with tons of energy ready for the day's lesson – applying makeup. The incredulous expression on each girl's face when she showed up not wearing makeup was always a favorite and made the session a lot of fun.

Most teens used way too much makeup in the daytime hours and she hoped to help them see that their youthful complexion and naturally beautiful skin needed very little help. It wasn't how much makeup but how and where applied that counted.

Annie had a shiny compact filled with the latest colors of eye shadow, blush, and an assortment of lip color at each girl's place. Estée Lauder was one of Like No Other's sponsors and not only did they donate the makeup for the program but had these adorable little cases specifically designed for each girl to take home.

"You'll have to share the mirrors. I only have six with me," she told the chatty group of teens. She glanced around the room and noticed Beth hadn't arrived. Annie felt terrible about the mix up and hoped she hadn't ruined things for Beth. She'd never lost any of her girls.

Beth never showed up and when Annie said goodbye to the last of her students, she drove to the RV Park.

Twenty minutes later she was knocking on the door of Dave Franklin's doublewide.

"Mr. Franklin. Would you give this to Beth? She wasn't at the session today and this is hers." She handed him the Estée Lauder case. "All the girls got one. It's part of the program. Please tell her I'll be happy to go over what she missed today—"

"It's all right, Dad. I'll talk to her." Dave moved aside as Beth stepped to the door.

"Oh. Hi Beth. We missed you today."

Beth folded her arms across her chest and stared back at her. Annie couldn't help but note the accusatory light in the teen's eyes.

"I'm sorry, Beth. For everything. I hope I didn't get you in trouble."

Beth glanced down, scuffed her toe against the door flashing, and shrugged. "It's okay. I'm over it. That's not why I wasn't there today. I went to an audition."

"What kind of audition?"

"Dance. It's for some Disney thing."

"Oh, my gosh. Beth, that's wonderful." So she was a dancer. That explained her grace and poise. Dancers made wonderful fashion models. "Well, I can't stay. I just wanted you to have your gift from today's workshop."

Beth gave a little finger wave, then closed the door.

Annie let out a deep sigh. It seemed Beth and her dad had forgiven her. Tomorrow she and Levi were flying to Des Moines to see her father where she would have a similar opportunity. In her heart she had already forgiven her father, but it was something else to actually say the words to his face. She hoped she had the courage to do so.

* * *

Annie and Levi followed a friendly staff member down the hallway of Columbia Health Center to the Family

Room, one of several small, private spaces set aside for those visiting a loved one.

Even though she was nervous, Annie took note of the clean but dated, green and yellow décor of the facility. Funny how one noticed the most mundane details in times of stress.

"You okay?" Levi asked.

She nodded.

"It's not too late if you want to call this off. I'll go tell him myself."

"No. I'm fine."

"Okay. I'll come in with you, and when you say the word I'll slip into the hallway and wait."

"But you'll stay if I want you to, right?"

"Right."

She'd told Levi she might need to see her father alone. That he might want to say something to her in private. Levi had balked at the idea but didn't argue. He'd been wonderful and she loved how he wanted to protect her.

The staff member paused outside the small room. "Here you are. Enjoy your visit."

When they entered, Frank Dell stood to greet them. Annie paused just inside the doorway. She hardly recognized the gaunt, hollow-eyed figure standing before her. Gone was the big, brawny, officer she'd remembered. Even in her low heels, she towered over him. Although in his late fifties, his thin, frail appearance made him look much older. She supposed alcohol abuse did that to people. Robbed them of their youth *and* their daughters.

"You've changed," he said. "All grown up and so like your mother."

"I take it that's okay with you now."

Frank visibly flinched. "Won't you both sit down?" he said.

They followed Frank to the small grouping and sat down on the sofa opposite him.

"I'm Frank Dell." He held out his hand to Levi who chose to ignore it.

"Levi Hawke."

Levi looked ready to murder him. She gave his hand a firm squeeze.

Annie clutched her purse in her lap and fought for something to say. "You've changed, too," she said.

He nodded. "It's been ten years. In the beginning, I searched for you, but later I stopped. I knew you didn't want to come home." He swallowed. "I know it's probably too late for your forgiveness." He glanced nervously at Levi, then back to her. "I was a drunken fool."

"You were a monster." She corrected him.

His hallow cheeks blanched. "You're right. There's no excuse for the way I treated you. But, I hope you'll forgive me."

Annie focused on her heartbeat and tried not to think about anything other than getting through this moment.

Frank Dell leaned forward and clasped his hands together. "This is the third time I've been in rehab. And you know what they say about third times." He laughed, a crotchety, pitiful sound.

"I truly hope it works for you this time." She glanced at Levi and squeezed his hand. "If you'd like to get a cup of coffee, I'll be fine."

For a moment she thought he was going to refuse, but he nodded and stood. His blue eyes narrowed as he stared down at her father. A silent signal perhaps? Then he left.

She focused on her father. "You know. I've often thought of what I'd say to you if I ever saw you again."

She thought about all the times she stood in front of her mirror and practiced for this moment. How she wove together the most clever and cutting words she could think of. How she compiled and ticked off the list of atrocities, reliving the humiliation and the heartache. But now that she had the opportunity she couldn't do it. And she realized she didn't need to, because he already knew. It was in his sorrow-filled, pitiful eyes.

Finding it difficult to look at him, she took a moment to glance out the window. "You were never a dad to me," she said. "And I'm sorry for that. That's all I ever wanted."

His eyes held pain and his face mirrored her own anxiety and she pitied him. "I forgive you."

She'd always thought the words would choke her, but instead a weight lifted. As if she'd been bound and tied, then suddenly released.

"Thank you. I know I don't deserve it, but I accept your forgiveness even though I suspect your heart's not in it."

"I've found that when you say something in faith, the heart usually follows," she said. "I forgave you a long time ago. It's the only way I've been able to make it."

It was true. Her years of therapy had led to forgiveness. And, today she'd faced the ultimate test. She'd looked her father and her demons square in the face and knew she was all right.

Relief filled his eyes. "I'm glad."

She stood. A small part of her hated to leave him. Which was crazy, considering. "I have to go. Our plane leaves in a couple of hours."

He rose to his feet, trembling slightly. "Of course."

They stared at each other in uncomfortable silence. She slipped her purse over her shoulder, gripped the strap, and swallowed. He took an awkward step toward her. It took everything ounce of courage to let him touch her. She gently placed her arms around him. His frail hands gripped her shoulders. When she stepped away, he had tears in his eyes.

"Goodbye." She walked to the doorway.

"Will I see you again?" he asked.

She turned around. "I hope you recover, but I can't promise any more than that." She'd done the right thing in coming here. She could now walk away, free to continue building her own life.

Annie left the sitting room and found Levi leaning against the opposite wall waiting for her. The lines of his handsome face were serious and thoughtful. Anger clouded his eyes. Not toward her but at the man in the other room. Levi had championed her. Protected her. In that moment she knew she loved him. She smiled. It seemed knights really did exist after all.

As soon as Levi noticed her, he pushed away from the wall and placed his hands along her arms. "You okay?"

"I'll admit. There's some pain. The whole time I was in there I kept thinking, why me? Why do some kids have a great dad and others don't?"

He pulled her in his arms. "Sometimes the world is a mixed up place," he said.

She nodded and linked her arm through his. They walked in silence down the hall, then through the wide foyer. Away from Frank Dell.

# Chapter Twenty-Seven

After class on the following Saturday, Annie pushed open the school doors to find *Orlando Times* reporter, Ethan Knight, waiting for her.

"Miss Dell."

Ethan Knight pushed off his car and stepped in her path, blocking her. Giving her no choice but to stop.

"I'm writing a follow up article on Like No Other and wondered if I could ask you a few questions."

"I'm sorry, but I'm late for an appointment." Wary, she stepped around him and hustled to her car.

He trotted after her. "This will only take a second."

She paused and turned to him. She didn't trust Ethan Knight. The last time he wrote about Like No Other, he focused on Alex Langdon's possible connection to the organization and nothing else. He was too eager, like a dog salivating over a bone.

"What is your relationship with Sheriff Hawke?"

"Excuse me?"

"I'm writing a special interest story. Using the sheriff's position as local chairman for Like No Other, as a sort of springboard to the sheriff's re-election campaign. You're well liked in this community and so is the sheriff. People love stories like this."

"I'm sorry. If you want to pose your questions to the sheriff, that's your business, but I have nothing to say." She gripped the door handle.

"Tell me what you know about Alex Langdon."

She heaved a sigh. "I'm afraid that's a question you'll have to direct to Like No Other's Board of Directors. This interview is over." She yanked on her door handle.

"Is everything all right, Annie?" Amanda exited the school and walked briskly toward them.

"Yes. Mr. Knight was just asking me some questions."

Amanda stopped right in front of Ethan Knight, folded her arms across her chest, and gave him what Annie assumed was her school principle *evil eye*.

Ethan Knight acknowledged Amanda with a brief nod. "*Miss* Marsh."

"Mr. Knight."

"So. You're the principal now?" he said.

"I am. And you, sir, are done here."

Annie watched this exchange in wonder.

Ethan's eyes filled with amusement, then he turned his attention to Annie. "I believe the principal has just dismissed me. Thank you for your time."

They watched him walk across the parking lot to his car. Annie turned to ask Amanda what *that* was all about, but at the fierce expression on her face, thought better of it. Instead she thanked Amanda for her timely intervention, then left. As she drove past Ethan Knight, he was sitting in his car, smiling like the Cheshire cat.

Annie's gut churned all the way to Cole's Oyster Bar. Ethan Knight was up to something. No doubt about that. She had the uncanny feeling he already knew more than he let on.

* * *

As soon as Annie walked in the restaurant, Levi could tell something was wrong. She looked rattled, her beautiful eyes clouded over. She sat down, gave him a brief smile that didn't reach her eyes.

"Have you forgotten something?" he asked.

She blinked at him.

"My, hey honey, how are you, kiss?"

"Sorry, darling." She stood up, gave a quick kiss then slid back in her seat.

"Let's see, if I were rating that kiss, I'd only give it three stars. And since when do you look at a menu?"

She closed it with a snap. "Sorry, I'm just preoccupied."

"What's the matter? Everything go all right with your workshop? Is it one of the girls?"

"No, no. We had a great time." Her words tumbled out. "Everything's fine."

*A lie.*

"Is it your father?"

"No." She hung her head and fiddled with her bracelet. "It's nothing really."

*Another lie.*

"Can you please drop it?" Her eyes pleaded.

He gazed at the face of the woman he'd come to love. She still had trust issues. Considering her background it was to be expected.

"So. How are my oysters going to be prepared today?" she asked, forcing a smile.

*And not very good at changing the subject.*

No sooner than the words were out, Cole set a large platter of raw oysters on the center of the table.

"No. Absolutely not. They look disgusting." She leaned across the table and got in his face. "If this is what I can expect on the third Saturday, what happens on the fourth? Do I have to catch them or something? Next, you'll be expecting me to shuck the darn things." Her eyes widened. "That's it, isn't it? You want me to shuck the nasty things."

He laughed. Distressed or not, she was so cute.

"You have to try them. Come on. Be brave." He forked one from the open shell it was sitting on, dipped it in the hot sauce, and shoved it in his mouth. "Mmmm."

She pulled a scrunched-up face, then folded her arms across her chest.

"No."

At that moment, Cole returned to their table with a plate of oysters Rockefeller. "Levi told me you weren't ready for the ultimate oyster eating experience so he ordered these for you. Enjoy, *ma petite*."

"Honestly, Levi. Sometimes I'm amazed that you're the town sheriff. I swear, there's a mischievous streak in you."

He chuckled and picked up a lemon wedge.

"Okay, this looks pretty good," she said. "But the verdict is out until I taste them."

"They're fantastic." He squeezed lemon juice over the hot, bubbling breadcrumbs and Parmesan cheese dish, forked a fat one, then lifted it to her mouth. "Add in spinach and shallots and you're in for a culinary treat."

Annie opened her pretty mouth and accepted the hot morsel.

"Okay, you're right." Her dimple peeked along with her smile. "They're good." She forked another one. "The best part is, they're cooked."

* * *

After lunch Levi told Annie to follow him in her car. They wound their way through town and ended up at the Green Parrot Bar and Grill, the restaurant where Annie pretended to pick up poor 'ole Phil. She pulled in beside his car and got out.

"I thought this place was only open in the evenings." She followed Levi to the front door.

He placed his key in the lock, then held the door for her. The restaurant was just as she'd remembered. Except for the lights that were on near the bar, the place was dark.

"What are we doing here?"

"I thought it was time I brought you to my place."

"Your place." She laughed. "You live in a restaurant?"

"I live above it." He pointed to the stairs he'd come down that night when he caught her with Phil.

As they made their way up the stairs, he took her hand in his.

"When I first came here from Fort Lauderdale, I didn't have a place to live. I got a job here waiting tables and washing dishes and the owner let me have this apartment as part of my pay. At the time, running for sheriff never entered my head."

"So you didn't have the job when you came here."

"That's right. I'd run away from a terrible situation."

She paused near the top step and gaped at him. He smiled, lifted his finger, and tapped her nose.

"You see? You're not the only one who's run away."

"That doesn't sound like you at all."

"I was twenty-four. A rookie cop."

At the top of the stairs he unlocked the door to his apartment.

"Wow, this is nice," she said. "Does it cover the entire upstairs?"

"Mostly. There's a storage room down the hall, but the rest is mine."

Annie walked around the space, while Levi made his way to the kitchen. The room was certainly masculine, cold even. But the leather sofa and metal furniture seemed perfect for Levi. Except for the bookcase and a seascape oil painting over the sofa, there wasn't much warmth.

Levi set two glasses on the counter, then glanced at her. "What do you think?"

"I think it needs a woman's touch." She threw over her shoulder.

"That could be arranged," he said.

As she sauntered through the open space, what enthralled her the most was his cop memorabilia. A collection of antique badges sat in a display case on a large square coffee table in the center of the room.

"These are amazing." She bent forward to take a closer look. Even though some were shiny and others dull, each badge had its own unique shape and size. They ranged from colorful to plain, but each its own little piece of art.

She ended her self-guided tour at the bookcase. Black and white photographs of famous sheriffs stared back at her from the shelves. She picked one up. "Who's this?"

"That's Buford Pusser, the famous Tennessee sheriff. He and my grandfather were in the same graduating class. He was a cop, too."

She turned to him and caught the merriment in his eyes. "Why am I not surprised?"

She continued to peruse the shelves until a photo of a younger Levi caught her attention. He had his arm around a cute teenage girl. They were both smiling at the camera.

"What a beautiful girl. Was she your girlfriend?"

He'd come up behind her with a couple of drinks.

"No. She was my younger sister."

She took the glass and gazed at him. His expression was sober and thoughtful. The corners of his mouth lifted slightly as he looked at the photo.

"That's right. You told me she passed away. I'm so sorry. How did it happen?" She took a sip of wine and waited.

He shook his head. "It was a long time ago."

She placed her free hand against his cheek and held it there until he lifted his gaze to hers. "I understand what it's like to hold tightly to a painful memory. Please tell me what happened?"

He nodded. "Let's sit down."

She followed him to the leather sofa and curled up next to him. His sober expression told her this was going to be difficult.

He glanced at her and she responded with what she hoped was an encouraging smile.

"I told you earlier that I came here looking for a job. That's because I was responsible for my sister's death."

"Oh no." She laid a comforting hand on his arm.

"I was a rookie cop with the Fort Lauderdale police Department. Had been on the job less than a year. I was on patrol on I 95. It was the end of March." He twisted his wine glass between his fingers. "My sister was a freshman at Florida State. She and two of her girlfriends were driving down for spring break. They were speeding and after I pulled them over, I discovered my kid sister was in the back seat."

Annie's heart sank. She knew what was coming.

"You can imagine the rest. I was the cocky young buck enjoying the flirty blonde and brunette in the front seat. And there was my nineteen-year-old sister, sitting in the back, pleading along with the other two, for me not to give the driver a ticket. I remember specifically, she pressed her hands together like she was praying."

Annie felt the blood drain from her face.

"Then she smiled," he said. "Just like in that photo. It's the last time I saw her alive."

"So. You gave them a warning and let them go."

He nodded. "Ten minutes later they were all dead. Apparently, the driver had been drinking and if I'd been doing my job instead of flirting and playing the jock, they would be alive today."

Annie thought about the day Levi pulled her over and how she'd brazenly flirted with him like he was some idiot she could manipulate. Shame washed over her. No wonder he'd been so put out with her.

She set her glass on the square table at her feet and slid her arms around Levi's shoulders. He folded her to him and held her there.

"I can't imagine what that must have done to you." She gave him a firm squeeze. "No wonder you were so angry with me that day. Please forgive me."

He squeezed her back, kissing her forehead.

"I left Fort Lauderdale after that. The pain was too great. My own parents had trouble looking at me. I had to get away. Start over. A different scene and all that. Over the years, I developed a harshness I can't say I'm proud of."

"It made you a tough sheriff."

"That it did. You get up in the morning, you get dressed and your entire demeanor changes. You wonder if the next car you pull over will be your last. You become quiet, stern and thoughtful, mentally preparing yourself for whatever the day may bring. You stop being you."

"Then you strap on your gun and become Robo Cop."

"That's right," he chuckled. "And don't you forget it."

"There's nothing wrong with being tough. No telling how many lives you've saved because of it. Maybe even mine."

"Then you came along and melted that rock hard block of ice. Thawed me out." He cupped her face in his hands. "You taught me that I can save lives *and* still have a heart."

"And your parents? How is it with them, now?"

He leaned back against the sofa and kept his arm over her shoulder. "It's good. They just needed time. I understood. They were heartbroken as any mom and dad would be losing a child."

"So how did you end up here?"

"It was as far away as I could get and still be in Florida. Plus, it was undeveloped as a tourist town, quiet and peaceful, which was what I needed."

"And then you became the sheriff and the rest as they say is history, right?"

"Something like that." He kissed the top of her head. "I met the man who was sheriff at the time right here in this restaurant. I was waiting tables and he recognized me from the news. He told me I wasn't the only cop who'd had a bad experience and that I was too talented to quit. He offered me a job as one of his deputies and I never waited tables again."

She snuggled closer and placed her hand on his thigh. "Thanks for telling me."

"I've wanted to since our trip to Des Moines." He ran his fingers through her hair. "I've kept it a secret for years. It's public record of course, so if anybody wanted to find out, they could. To my knowledge, no one here knows anything about it, and with the upcoming election, I'd like to keep it that way."

"Of course, I understand."

"I just don't want their pity. That was why I left Fort Lauderdale. I could see it in their eyes, from everyone in the department, to my friends."

She finished her wine and set the glass on the memorabilia coffee table. "That's one reason I never told anyone about how my father treated me. Not so much when it was happening. That was for pure fear. But later on, I just didn't want their pity."

"Then you started volunteering for Like No Other," he said. "I understand now why it's been so important for you not to lose this opportunity. These girls, the foundation, mean so much because of what happened to you."

She nodded. Should she tell him her connection was more than that? That Like No Other was her brainchild, her baby? She thought about the first little group of girls she'd worked with in New York. At the time it didn't even have a name. Just a few sessions with a group of inner city teen girls that had signed up through their church.

"I like your place." She slipped the wine glass from his fingers and placed it on the low table, then pecked his cheek. "Thanks for bring me here." She pushed against his shoulders until he was lying back on the sofa and she was on top of him. "I hope it's a sign of more to come."

"Oh you do, do you?"

"Mmm-Hum." She kissed his warm lips and tasted a hint of wine.

"My but you're a forward little thing," he said.

"Not at all, Sheriff. You'd know it if I were forward. I'd say something like, 'When am I going to meet your mother?' And then you'd say, 'How about Sunday afternoon for dinner. She makes the most tender pot roast.' Then I'd say—"

He kissed her. A shut your mouth, heart pounding kiss that melted her bones. If he only knew how much she did want to meet his mother and to belong to him forever.

# Chapter Twenty-Eight

Bang! Annie jerked awake. What the heck? The pounding continued and pulled her from the dregs of sleep. She glanced at the little pink wall clock. 7:30 a.m. She lifted the islet curtain and peeked out the window. It was Levi. She sucked in an excited breath, leapt out of bed and in three short steps, wrenched open the door.

"Hey you." Her smile froze as he pushed his way in. "What's wrong? What happened?"

He slapped the *Orlando Times* on her Formica counter. "Is this how you respect my confidence?"

His eyes blazed, hot and molten. She swallowed and stepped to the counter. The newspaper headline jumped off the page.

LOCAL SHERIFF DATES ALEX LANGDON'S EX.

"Oh, God." She clutched her pajama top and gazed in horror at Levi. He was stone faced and a muscle twitched in his clenched jaw.

"How did this happen?"

"As if you don't know." His voice was low and in control.

"Levi, I—"

"First, Franklin, and now me." He looked ready to explode but held his anger in check. "No one in this community will ever see me the same way again. Do you even realize what you've done?"

"What are you talking about?" she wailed. "What do you mean?"

"Or is it just an example of your hatred for cops?"

"Levi, please."

"Yes, you'd better beg. This time you've gone too far. I suggest you read the entire article. Your photographer friends are already swarming our town." He turned on his heel and was gone.

"Levi, wait!"

She threw her hands over her mouth and watched him drive away, tires spitting gravel and pine needles everywhere.

With shaking hands, she picked up the *Orlando Times* and began reading the article. Her stomach churned until she thought she might throw up. Somehow Ethan Knight had uncovered her real identity, discovered her connection to Alex Langdon and his financial link as treasurer to Like No Other. At least he didn't uncover her true connection to LNO but it was no telling what the Board would do when they found out about this. That she could handle, but it was the caption near the end of the article about Levi and his sister that made her ill.

*Local Sheriff Responsible for Sister's Death. Re-election Now Slim.*

Her legs buckled and she collapsed on the sofa. Levi had spent years rebuilding his life. And, for what? So this jerk could have a story. She wrapped her arms around her torso. How could Levi think she'd betray him like this? Pain pierced her heart.

Her cell phone rang and she jumped. Hoping it was Levi, she checked the caller ID, but it was Randal Kennedy, the board chairman of Like No Other. Her stomach plummeted. She knew what was coming. "Hello, Randy."

"Anna, you know I have no choice. I'm terribly sorry, but in light of the news that broke this morning, I'm asking you to step down from all involvement with LNO. The board knows you're not involved with Alex Langdon's criminal acts but we have to protect the organization. Any hint of possible criminal misconduct would destroy everything you've built so far."

"I understand and I agree with you." She placed a shaking hand to her forehead. "I have one more Saturday with the girls, here. You'll need to send someone else to finish. I don't want these young women affected by what's happened."

That afternoon, Annie hoisted the last of her belongings in the mini coup and shut the hatch. She stopped on her way out to pay Pete for the last week and hugged him goodbye. She slid back behind the wheel, buckled her seat belt, and left the RV Park for good.

* * *

Annie sat in the window seat overlooking New York City. Another cold and dreary fall day in the big apple. She shivered and pulled her chenille robe tightly around her. She leaned against the long windowpane and stared at the tall, grey buildings that seemed to go on forever. She missed her little trailer and her single palm tree. She missed the girls and Levi most of all.

For the past two weeks, Alex Langdon, Anna Delany, and Like No Other were splattered all over the national news. But yesterday, seemingly out of nowhere, there had been a breakthrough in the investigation. Alex Langdon copped a plea deal and confessed everything, from his fraudulent investment schemes to laundering money through his own business. Apparently, the funds for Like

No Other had never been touched, clearing Anna Delany's name in the minds and hearts of the public, once and for all.

The board had reinstated her and told her it was time the world knew of her real involvement in the charitable organization. After their announcement, sponsors came out of the woodwork. A major TV Network offered her a reality show about her work with the organization.

But none of that mattered. It seemed all she was good for lately was to sit and brood and stare out the window. In hopes of what? That he would miraculously show up at her door?

Door chimes rang through her apartment. Her heart leapt and pounded. She sat perfectly still for the briefest moment, then shot off the bench to wrench open the door.

Tony, the apartment doorman, stood in front of her. "Here's your mail."

"Oh, thanks, Tony."

"You okay?"

She shrugged "I'm getting there." She waved the stack of mail through the air. "Thanks for bring this up."

"No problem." He tipped his fingers to his forehead and left.

She leaned against the doorjamb and watched him go down the stairs. "Hey, Tony!"

He paused about half way down and turned back.

"How come you don't ever use the elevator?"

He patted his fifty-something, protruding belly and grinned. "The stairs keep me fit." He waved and continued down the steps.

Annie shook her head and closed the door. She padded over to the window seat and flipped through the *Elle* Magazine, pausing at the latest Banning ad that now belonged to someone else. The model sported glorious red hair and flawless skin. She was a good choice for the skin and hair care company. Bravo for them. She shut the magazine and tossed it on the floor.

The doorbell pealed, again. "Now what?"

She marched over to the door and yanked it open. A man dressed like a chef stood in her doorway behind a food cart. He was wearing a white coat with the name, *Le Cirque*, stitched over his left pocket. A very large silver dome-covered dish sat in the center of the cart along with a chilled bottle of wine.

"Miss Delany?"

"Yes?"

"I have lunch for you."

"I'm sorry, but I didn't order this."

"I believe it's a gift. Where would you like it?"

"Um, over there is fine." She waved her arm toward the window seat, then held the door while he pushed the cart through the opening.

"Who is it from?"

"The gentleman wished to remain anonymous."

She stepped over to a side table and drew her wallet from her purse.

"It's already been taken care of, miss," he said, while setting up the table. "When you're finished, call this number and we'll come get it." He handed her a business card, then left.

Annie perused the table for a card or some other identification, but there was nothing. Hum. Maybe it was from Alex. An, 'I'm sorry I screwed up your life' gift. This was exactly the kind of thing he would do.

She looked at the shiny dome wondering what was underneath. She was rather hungry. She hadn't eaten much since…well, since she'd returned to New York. She sat down, unwrapped the silver flatware from the napkin, then reached for the dome.

The door rang, and she sat back in exasperation. "Seriously?" She tossed the napkin on the table, stalked over to the door, then yanked it open.

Sheriff Levi Hawke stood smack dab in front of her. In her doorway. In New York City. All masculine, and fine and devastatingly attractive in a navy blue suit. He gazed down at her with a question his eyes.

"May I come in?"

She didn't think she'd ever hear that deep, familiar, voice again. She nodded and stepped back so he could enter, never once taking her eyes from his face.

"Thank you." He clutched a bouquet of flowers in his hand. "After the way I treated you, I fully expected to have the door slammed in my face."

Annie knew she should say something but all she could do was stand there and stare. She hadn't seen him dressed up since Liddy's wedding and he was utterly gorgeous.

"These are for you." He handed her the bouquet of pink tulips.

To stall for more time, she pressed her nose into the lush bouquet and inhaled. She was shaking internally and couldn't believe he was standing in her apartment. Was this really happening? Did he actually come back for her? She lifted her face. "They're beautiful."

"So are you. Without makeup and in your pink, plaid, flannel pajamas, you are the most beautiful woman I've ever seen. Will you forgive me?"

She hesitated, wondering what made him change his mind. She knew the article had hurt him and yet here he was, flowers in hand. She caught her lower lip between her teeth. She stared into his face, noticed the furrow between his eyes and had the strongest desire to kiss it away.

"Yes," she whispered, then flew into his arms.

* * *

"I was a fool." He held her tightly, reveling in the feel of her. "I should have trusted you. Instead, I blamed you."

She tilted her head and placed her fingers over his mouth. "Don't say another word. Just kiss me."

He drank in her loveliness. Her radiant face and the warmth in her glowing brown eyes moved across his beating heart like a love song. His lips claimed hers and she melted against him.

A few moments later she led him over to the window seat. They sat down with New York City sprawled behind them. Annie grasped his hand in her small one.

"I'm so sorry about the article, and your sister, and everything. I still feel terrible about it."

"It's not your fault." He loved the feel of her small velvet hand in his. "It was never your fault. Ethan Knight did his own investigation. I told you before, that accident was public information so it wasn't hard for him to find."

She stared at her lap. "I know, but if I hadn't come to town none of this would have happened."

"Don't say that." He lifted her chin with his hand. "You can't live your life in hindsight. None of us can. I think we've both learned that the past few weeks. Besides." He wrapped his arms around her and drew her to him. "I can't imagine living one more day without you."

Her sparkling brown eyes glistened with adoration and his heart soared.

"And, truthfully, I'm glad everyone knows. It's frankly a weight off my shoulders. It had ruled my life and clouded my thinking far too long."

"And the election?"

"I don't know. But, if the Franklin County voters chose someone else…" He shrugged. "So be it. You are more important to me than any election."

Annie sighed and relaxed against him. "I had almost given up on you ever coming for me."

"I would have been here sooner, but I had something to take care of first. And I'm ashamed to say, it took me a few days before I realized what a fool I'd been. Mark and Liddy returned shortly after you left and I hashed the entire story out with them. Then Liddy lay into me like a mama wildcat protecting her cub."

Annie leaned back to look fully at him. "Reamed you out, did she?"

"He laughed. "That's one way to say it."

He placed his mouth over hers and kissed her. "When I went back to your place, ready to grovel, you were gone."

"After what happened, I couldn't stay. Plus, I was fired from Like No Other."

"I know. The girls were terribly disappointed you couldn't finish with them."

"How'd the other model work out?"

"She was great. But they missed you."

"I missed them, too."

She snuggled against his chest and he ran his hand gently over the top of her head. "I'm so proud of you."

She raised her eyes to his. "What for?"

"I know you're the founder of Like No Other. I know everything."

"Then you know about Alex's confession."

"I do."

She pushed herself upright. "So. Now I'm okay for you to be around? Is that it?"

"No. That is not it." He took hold of her chenille and flannel-covered arms and turned her toward him. "I paid a visit to your friend, Alex, and convinced him it would be to his benefit to tell the world the truth."

Her jaw dropped and her eyes filled with something close to admiration.

"It seems he has a bit of a conscience after all," Levi said.

"What did you say to him?"

"I gave him my best Dirty Harry impression."

"You *are* Buford Pusser."

"Hardly." He laughed. "Actually, I retained a lawyer who spoke eloquently on your behalf." He smiled down at her happy, glowing face. "He needed little convincing to protect you and assured the authorities you had no knowledge of his fraudulent activities."

She sighed and gazed adoringly up at him.

"But, enough of singing my praises. Let's eat."

She glanced at the small table at her elbow and raised a delicate brow. "This is from you?"

"It is." He chuckled. "You and I have some unfinished business to attend to."

"That sounds ominous."

With a grand gesture, he lifted the lid.

"Oh, no. You've got to be kidding."

"You left town before I could give you your final lesson. Cole was disappointed, I might add."

"This is not what I'd call a make-up dinner." She gazed with apprehension at the display of oysters on the half shell.

Levi dotted a raw oyster with Louisiana Hot Sauce and watched her face scrunch up in disgust.

"Come on." He coaxed. "Don't eat with your eyes."

"Okay. Fine."

"Open wide."

Annie complied and Levi slid the raw oyster between her lips.

Annie bit into the textured mollusk and swallowed. "You actually like this?"

"Really?" He sat back against the cushion. "You didn't like it?"

"I didn't. But, I didn't actually hate it, either," she confessed.

"Okay, let me try one." Levi splashed the mollusk with hot sauce and placed it in his mouth. A slight bitter, metallic taste mingled with salt and brine shimmied across his tongue. "Delicious."

She grimaced.

"You really didn't like it?" he asked.

She shook her head.

"I suspected that would be the case." Levi leaned forward and pulled out another dome-covered plate from the lower shelf, which had been hidden underneath the tablecloth. "Would you rather have the Shrimp Scampi?"

"More seafood." Annie punched him in the arm. "Wonderful." She teased, leaning in for his kiss. "Have you ever heard of red meat and potatoes?"

"Funny you should mention that," he said. "Next Sunday, we're having pot roast at my mother's."

"Really?"

"Yes, but first, I have to ask you a question."

"Okaaay."

"Anna Marie Dell–Delany."

Annie's eyes grew round and she placed her hands over her heart.

"Please hold out your left hand."

She held out her hand, then quickly pulled it back to her chest. "You're not going to cuff me again are you?"

A smiled peeked at the corners of her mouth and her deep golden eyes sparkled with anticipation. God, he loved her.

"In a manner, yes." He held her gaze as he slipped an emerald ring from his pocket. "But, I think this is a much better way to keep you by my side."

"Oh, Levi."

He slipped the ring onto her third finger, then raised her hand to his lips.

"It's beautiful," she said.

"I love you, Annie." He drew her in his arms and kissed her. Thoroughly and completely. The oysters and shrimp momentarily forgotten.

*Thank you for reading!*

Dear Reader,

I hope you enjoyed ***Hawke's Nest: Like No Other Book 1***. And if you're wondering what's going on between Amanda Marsh and Ethan Knight, you'll be able to find out in ***Like No Other Book 2***.

I need to ask a favor. As you probably know, reviews can be hard to come by. And as a reader your feedback is so important. If you're so inclined, I'd love an honest review of Hawke's Nest. It doesn't have to be long or fancy. :) One or two sentences is fine.

If you have time, here's a link to my author page on Amazon. You can check out all my books here: amazon.com/-/e/B0077AG3ZM

In gratitude,

*Darcy Flynn*

# About the Author

Darcy Flynn's life is a gumbo world. Take a little New Orleans heritage, some art, music, dance and add a lot of love and time to simmer and all you have is spice, flavor, and a memory of something so fine you can't wait for another helping. Her fiction is a few B&Bs, a bit of moon magic and a lot of problems mixed with a healthy portion of sweet romance. Add a dash of sizzle and a lot of sass and all that's left is magic. Her refreshing storylines, irritatingly handsome heroes and feisty heroines will delight and entertain you from the first page to the last.

A native of New Orleans, Darcy swapped her city roots for garden boots when she and her husband moved to their farm in Franklin, Tennessee, where Darcy is surrounded by her beautiful gardens and a menagerie of living creatures–English setters and Millie Fleur chickens, being her favorite.

Although, published in the Christian non-fiction market under her real name, Joy Dent, it was the empty nest that turned her to writing romantic fiction. Proving that it's never too late to follow your dreams.

Please follow Darcy on Twitter: @darcyflynn
and visit her website: darcyflynnromances.com
to sign up for her newsletter,
or feel free to drop her a line at:
darcyflynnromances@gmail.com.

9 781941 925003